PRAISE FOR IAN RANKIN

'The themes that would come to dominate the Rebus books are already here in embryonic form: the blurred boundaries between good and evil; the pull of superstition and myth; the difficulties in escaping and resolving one's past; the emotional complexities of the male of the species; and, not least, a good mystery' *Time Out*

'Full of secrets and revelations, with an atmospheric sense of time and place, it has Rankin's signature darkness. A young man's book – and the start of something big' *Choice*

'Rankin's talent is clear, even in this uneven early work, and *The Flood*'s use of Scottish mythology is clever. The depiction of the single mother at the book's heart is often finely drawn and always sympathetic . . . There is, too, a real tension to its closing chapters' John Connolly, *Irish Times*

'The book can now be regarded as a kind of historical artefact, taking us back to the London of the 1980s . . . *Watchman* is one for Rankin aficionados, interesting in itself, but also revealing as to a direction he might have taken with his fiction'

Keith Jeffery, *TLS*

'The Rebus books, with their atmospheric urban Scottish locales, have an iron-clad following, but Rebus fans will find something very different here . . . a very impressive piece of work . . . If you're worried you'll miss the comfortable presence of John

Rebus, don't – this is totally involving stuff, delivered with the kind of panache that hallmarks the Edinburgh-set thrillers. Miles is a strongly drawn character . . . Even if the espionage genre was a blind alley for Rankin, he unquestionably had its measure'
Barry Forshaw, *Daily Express*

'It is intriguing to compare it with his Rebus books . . . a must. Layers of intrigue are peeled away'
Glasgow Evening Times

'Rankin is a master at what, for me, is one of the important aspects of a crime novel: the integration of setting, plot, characters and a theme which, for Rankin, is the moral dimension never far from his writing' *Guardian*

'Crimemaster Rankin is back . . . a powerful book brimming with genuine social comment'
Sunday Express

'Rankin is streets ahead in the British police procedural writing field' *Independent on Sunday*

'Rebus is a masterful creation . . . Rankin has taken his well-earned place among the top echelon of crimewriters' *Observer*

'His prose is as vivid and terse as the next man's yet its flexibility and rhythm give it potential for lyrical expression which is distinctly Rankin's own'
Scotland on Sunday

Born in the Kingdom of Fife in 1960, Ian Rankin graduated from the University of Edinburgh in 1982, and then spent three years writing novels when he was supposed to be working towards a PhD in Scottish Literature. His first Rebus novel, *Knots and Crosses*, was published in 1987, and the Rebus books are now translated into over thirty languages and are bestsellers worldwide.

Ian Rankin has been elected a Hawthornden Fellow, and is also a past winner of the Chandler-Fulbright Award. He is the recipient of four Crime Writers' Association Dagger Awards including the prestigious Diamond Dagger in 2005 and in 2009 was inducted into the CWA Hall of Fame. In 2004, Ian won America's celebrated Edgar Award for *Resurrection Men*. He has also been shortlisted for the Anthony Awards in the USA, and won Denmark's *Palle Rosenkrantz* Prize, the French *Grand Prix du Roman Noir* and the *Deutscher Krimipreis*. Ian Rankin is also the recipient of honorary degrees from the universities of Abertay, St Andrews, Edinburgh, Hull and the Open University.

A contributor to BBC2's *Newsnight Review*, he also presented his own TV series, *Ian Rankin's Evil Thoughts*. He has received the OBE for services to literature, opting to receive the prize in his home city of Edinburgh. He has also recently been appointed to the rank of Deputy Lieutenant of Edinburgh, where he lives with his partner and two sons. Visit his website at www.ianrankin.net

BY IAN RANKIN

The Inspector Rebus series

Knots and Crosses
Hide and Seek
Tooth and Nail
Strip Jack
The Black Book
Mortal Causes
Let It Bleed
Black and Blue
The Hanging Garden
Death Is Not the End (*novella*)
Dead Souls
Set in Darkness
The Falls
Resurrection Men
A Question of Blood
Fleshmarket Close
The Naming of the Dead
Exit Music

The Inspector Fox series

The Complaints
The Impossible Dead

Other novels

The Flood
Watchman
Westwind
Doors Open

Writing as Jack Harvey

Witch Hunt
Bleeding Hearts
Blood Hunt

Short stories

A Good Hanging and Other
    Stories
Beggars Banquet

Non-fiction

Rebus's Scotland

Omnibus editions

Rebus: The Early Years
(Knots and Crosses,
Hide and Seek, Tooth and Nail)

Rebus: The St Leonard's Years
(Strip Jack, The Black Book,
Mortal Causes)

Rebus: The Lost Years
(Let It Bleed, Black and Blue,
The Hanging Garden)

Rebus: Capital Crimes
(Dead Souls, Set in Darkness,
The Falls)

All Ian Rankin's titles are available on audio.

Also available: *Jackie Leven Said*
by Ian Rankin and Jackie Leven.

IAN RANKIN

THE FLOOD

For my father and mother

An Orion paperback

First published in Great Britain in 1986
by Polygon
This paperback edition published in 2006
by Orion Books Ltd,
Orion House, 5 Upper St Martin's Lane,
London WC2H 9EA

An Hachette UK company

Reissued 2012

A CIP catalogue record for this book
is available from the British Library.

Printed and bound in Great Britain by
Clays Ltd, St Ives plc

The Orion Publishing Group's policy is to use papers
that are natural, renewable and recyclable products and
made from wood grown in sustainable forests. The logging
and manufacturing processes are expected to conform to
the environmental regulations of the country of origin.

www.orionbooks.co.uk

Many waters cannot quench love, neither
can the floods drown it.   *Song of Songs*

All one's inventions are true.   *Flaubert*

INTRODUCTION

The Flood was my first published novel. It's not a crime novel, though it contains secrets and revelations. Nor is it a thriller. Fair warning: it's a young man's book, all about the perils and pitfalls of growing up.

I wrote it when I was a student at Edinburgh University. I have the feeling it started life as a short story, only the story started to grow. Before I knew it, I had written a full twenty pages – too long for Radio 4's short story slot (for which two of my stories had already been accepted), or for most of the magazines and other outlets for 'shorties' that I knew of at the time. I decided that instead of trying to edit what I already had, I should just call it 'part one' and keep going. I'd already written one novel, entitled *Summer Rites*, a black comedy set in a hotel in the Scottish Highlands. The plot revolved around a one-legged schizophrenic librarian, a young boy with special powers, and the abduction of a famous American novelist by the 'provisional wing' of the Scottish National Party. Curiously, no one had seemed to agree with my judgment that *Summer Rites* was a fully realised contender for the title of Great Scottish Novel. Undaunted, I set about turning my short story *The Falling Time* into a new novel called *The Flood*.

I was reading a lot of Scottish literature at the time, as part of my PhD study into the novels of Muriel Spark. Looking at *The Flood* now, I can see influences peering back at me: Neil Gunn, Iain Crichton Smith, and especially Robin Jenkins (author of the marvellous *The Cone Gatherers*). Although *The Flood* was written in the mid-1980s, at a time when a fresh urban Scottish fiction was arriving – thanks to writers such as James Kelman – I decided that my own story would be local and rural, based in and around a fictitious coal-mining community. The problem was, I named my village Carsden, which is why a lot of people back in my hometown of Cardenden thought I was writing about them. It hardly helped that the main character was called Sandy – the name of one of my school-friends – or that when I took the finished novel home to show my father, he perused the opening sentence and told me a woman called Mary Miller lived just over the back fence from him.

Turned out, I hadn't disguised the place of my birth well enough.

Up to this point, I'd been writing a lot of 'shorties', very few of them ever picked up for publication. However, I'd had some success with a story called *Walking Naked*, which had been based on an actual event from my family's history. In similar fashion, the original idea behind *The Flood* had been to describe a single scene – the moment when an aunt of mine (my father's sister; a mere girl at the time) had fallen into a stream composed of hot waste water from the washing-plant of the local coal-mine. She sported long hair, of which she was inordinately proud. A young man saved her by hauling her out of the stream by that same coil of hair. It was a tale my father had told me, probably embellishing it for effect.

I would embellish it further.

My first attempts at writing, back in my teenage years, had concerned my hometown. I'd written a long, rambling poem (a homage of sorts to T. S. Eliot) about the derelict Rex Cinema, some short stories based on incidents real and imaginary, and even a novella (written in filched school jotters), in which the plot of William Golding's *Lord of the Flies* was played out not on a desert island but in my high school. I was trying to mythologise the place, to give it a sense of importance at odds with the reality. With the coal-mines redundant, I'd watched some of the life (and livelihood) seep out of the place. As a student, I would spend weekdays in Edinburgh, and most weekends back home in Cardenden, taking my dad for a drink at the Bowhill Hotel, meeting friends from my schooldays at the Auld Hoose. I was trying to fit in, while becoming increasingly aware that I was moving further away from my roots all the time. In Edinburgh, I'd be reading *Paradise Lost* and *Ulysses*; back home, I'd be playing games of pool and discussing the previous week's John Peel playlists.

Maybe *The Flood* was part of the leaving process.

As well as reading a lot of Scottish literature, I'd also been reading about folklore and witchcraft, and catching up on literary effects such as symbolism. In fact, there was more in the final draft of the book than even I was aware of, as I discovered when, for a short time, *The Flood* became a set text for the university's Scottish Literature department. I was invited to sit in on a tutorial, with my identity being kept secret for the first half of the session – as far as the students were concerned, I was just a newcomer, albeit one a few years older than them. One student (I think he was American) delivered a paper on the book's wasteland imagery; another discussed Old and New Testament themes and borrowings, while a third had made a detailed study of the author's use of elements and colours. I started taking notes at one point: it was all good stuff! Even if I had not consciously meant for these patterns to exist, I was happy to acknowledge them if readers could see them. (I was a fan of the literary theorist Wolfgang Iser – eventually using his name for a Professor in my first Rebus novel. Iser's thesis was that it's what readers see in books that is important, not what the writer intended them to see. The name for this is Reader Response Criticism.)

I finished the final draft of *The Flood* on Monday 9 July 1984, having started it in January. During that first half of 1984 I was studying hard – everything from Proust to Derrida – and writing a lot, amassing a slew of rejection letters in the process. Some of these were from publishers, some from agents, and yet others from magazines, short story collections and competitions. Still I kept slogging, hungry for recognition as a writer. Iain Crichton Smith, having beaten me into second place in a short story contest run by the *Scotsman* newspaper, had written a letter of introduction to his publisher, Gollancz. But his editor, Livia Gollancz, had already turned down *Summer Rites*, and would reject *The Flood*, too. At the university, writer-in-residence Allan Massie had helped me to meet a London-based editor called Euan Cameron (who would eventually sign up *Knots & Crosses* to his publishing house, Bodley Head). But Euan wanted neither *Summer Rites* nor *The Flood*.

In the end, and unwittingly, it was James Kelman who helped me get published. The students at Edinburgh University ran their own publishing house. It was called Polygon and employed two or three full-time staff, complemented by any number of jobbing, unpaid students. Despite its lack of size and resources, however, Polygon had achieved fame and success with the publication of James Kelman's first collection of short stories, *Not Not While the Giro*. On the lookout for new authors, I became one of the lucky ones. Launching an imprint called 'Polygon New Writers', I found myself signed up with two other first-time authors, Robert Alan Jamieson and Alex Cathcart. And even though only a few hundred copies of *The Flood* would be printed, I can still remember the thrill of walking into the Polygon office on Buccleuch Place to sign my first-ever book contract. By coincidence, that same day (Tuesday 19 March 1985) I got the idea for another book, to be called *Knots & Crosses*. It would feature a troubled detective who would, in time, even meet one of the main characters in *The Flood*. (Check out the opening pages of *Hide & Seek* if you don't believe me.)

The Flood was edited by a fellow literature student called Iain Cameron, and proof-read by one of my lecturers. The painting on the jacket was provided by a student at the nearby art college. (A few years back, when Polygon was moving premises, I tried tracking down the original artwork, but it seemed to have vanished without trace.) The handsomely produced book was eventually published in February 1986, in a joint run of hardcover (three hundred) and paperback (maybe eight hundred). One of my diary entries of the time states: 'Saw "Flood" (and the other new Polygons) in Stockbridge Bookshop: it looked as though only one copy (of Alan Jamieson's novel) had been bought. Felt a twinge of failure.' However, the next day I was doing some tutoring at the university, and two of my students had brought copies of the book that they wanted me to sign. (I hope they've held on to them – *The Flood* has become highly collectable . . . and very expensive as a result, which explains this new edition – I want it to be available to everyone who wants it, without them needing to remortgage their house or pawn the children.)

Publication week climaxed with a launch party for all three authors held in one of the university buildings. I was photographed, had to read from the book in public for the first time, and even sold and signed a few copies. Afterwards, a bunch of friends took me to the Café Royal for a night of riotous assembly which ended with us being asked to leave.

I woke up next morning on a living-room floor, with my publication cheque (£300) safe in my pocket. It was a shaking, whey-faced author who posed that afternoon for a photographer from the *Dundee Courier*.

A trickle of reviews eventually arrived, as did a trickle of sales. By the end of May, I was recording in my diary that I'd sold five hundred copies in total. Meantime, an aunt of mine had finished reading the book and thought me depraved. According to my dad, she was 'crying for my soul'. If only she'd been a reviewer, some extra interest might have been drummed up. Eventually, I visited her in the flesh, so she could chastise me properly for writing such sordid stuff – 'all soiled knickers and fag-ends', I believe she said. She also asked how I would feel if my niece were to read the book. Little did she realise that I was already at work on my next project, which, in the fag-end stakes, would make *The Flood* look like *Little Women* . . .

1963–1969

The Falling Time

1985

Sandy

1985

The Flood

1963–1969
The Falling Time

1

When Mary Miller was ten years old and not yet a witch, and Carsden was still a thriving mining village, she would watch her brother Tom playing football in the park with his friends. She was attracted, young though she was, to their swagger, to the way they rolled their shirtsleeves up like their fathers and shouted for every ball. She would sit by the goalposts between which her brother danced and would console him when he let in a goal.

At that time she had a doll called Missie Lizzie, and she would clutch Missie Lizzie to her tiny chest as if sustaining her. The sun shone low over long summer evenings and the rumble of the pit-head lulled her into near sleep. Smoke drifted over the park while locomotives slipped away over distant rails. There was a rhythm to everything in those days, as if some tune were being played behind a veil beyond which the young girl could not see. The trees beside the hot burn snapped their fingers, and the lapping of the burn itself added the final cadence to the symphony.

One evening Mary was sitting against the iron fence behind Tom's goalposts, he having gone to the centre of the pitch to share in the half-time refreshments, and was falling asleep as usual with Missie Lizzie lying across her lap. The air was so clear that bird-calls seemed to carry to her ears from way over past the Auld Kirk and even Blackwood's Farm, and these were the sounds to which she fell asleep. She was a small, skinny thing with long black hair tied back into a ponytail which fell tantalisingly down her back and which, consequently, her brother Tom in one of his moods would often pull. Every hair would cry out as if burning when he did this, and she would run crying to her mother who would tell her father who would scold the bully, perhaps even letting him taste his pit-belt. Then Tom would not speak to her for a day or two, and would give her killing looks. Not today, though; there could be nothing but innocence in the park on such an evening. She could almost feel the warmth of the hot burn behind her, bringing its murky deposits down from the pit-head to be washed into the River Ore and carried out to sea. In the winter, steam rose from the hot burn and people warmed themselves beside it, some even waggling their fingers or bared toes in the dark liquid to revive the feeling in them. Sometimes the burn was red in colour, sometimes black, and occasionally a clearer bluey-grey, but only when the pit was idle.

Mary had been sleeping for only a few minutes when she found herself edging towards wakefulness because of some sounds nearby. There was a rustling and a faint whistling behind her, then muffled sniggers and more rustling. She knew, as she opened her eyes, that something was behind her, creeping through the field across which the hot burn threaded its course, nearing the railings against which she now sat petrified. From her still bleary eyes she could just make out Tom in the centre of the football pitch. He was laughing and biting into a half-orange. He would save a piece for her. The sounds were coming nearer, but she was too afraid to scream. Her mother had told her of the goblins who lived in the hot burn and would eat any young children who wandered close to their home without taking an adult for protection. Tom had laughed and told her that it was all a fairy story to stop her from going too close to the burn and maybe falling in. But perhaps, she now thought, she really had strayed too close to the goblins' home. Perhaps if she edged away now it would be all right.

Suddenly something growled immediately behind her and an arm, very human in design, snaked through the iron railings and snatched Missie Lizzie from Mary's lap. She screamed and stood up. The boys were whooping and careering across the field, tossing the doll between them. Mary was horrified. She screamed a high-pitched squeal and squeezed between the iron bars, almost getting stuck but eventually forcing herself through. Tom was shouting at her as she stumbled through the barley, which prickled her legs terribly. She made relentlessly towards the two boys, who seemed quite keen for her to follow. They were older boys, older even than Tom, and she recognised both of them. They grinned at her and waved Missie Lizzie towards her, and she was bawling with the tears threatening to blind her. She held out her arms towards Missie Lizzie as she walked towards her tormentors. When she was too close, the boys darted around her and trotted a little distance away. They waved the doll and laughed and jeered at her, and all the time she could hear Tom's voice angrily behind her as he tried to climb over the fence.

'I want it back, I want it back!' she cried as she reached out her arms. The doll, with its smiling stupid face and its red dress, was hanging high in the air now, was pinned by an adolescent arm against the deepening blue sky below which the hot burn murmured. She stood on tiptoe, ignoring the boy and his outstretched arm, and just touched Missie Lizzie's foot with her fingertips. The doll was released, and a soft push in Mary's back was all that was needed to send her toppling into the hot burn, screaming as she hit the water, taking in a choking mouthful of silt and heat and darkness. Her eyes stung as if sand had been thrown into her face. She knew that she should not be here. She gasped, feeling her hand breaking the surface of the water and touching the floating body of her doll. There was a swirling and a rushing and a bubbling of liquid. She had no right to be in this place. This was a warm dying place and dark. Her knees touched the gritty, yielding bottom, her hands in light and air and her body submerged. It was quite pleasant, really, to be away from the teasing boys and their cruelty. She began to give herself to the thick water. Then her hair was screaming, rough things clawing at it. There were goblins in the hot burn and she had disturbed their nest. She opened her eyes, but was blind. Then, hair screaming still, she felt herself rising from the liquid. Her hair was on fire, and suddenly she was in brightness and air and was being sick, spewing up all the silt and the darkness. She was dragged to the bank and her hair stopped screaming. Voices rushed into her ears as the water rushed out. 'By Christ, Tom, that was close.' 'Aye, pulled her out by the pigtail.' 'She was down there a while, though.' 'Are you all right, Mary?' 'I saw them. It was Matty Duncan and Jock McLeod's boy.' 'Is she all right there, Tom? Should we fetch your mum?'

Her dress clung to her like the dress of a rag-doll. Her stomach hurt and her eyes hurt and her head hurt, and she was shaking and crying and was afraid. She felt Tom touch her face, then she opened her eyes.

Her mother listened to the story and then told her to go upstairs and change; she would be up in a minute to help her. Mary left her mother with Tom and climbed the narrow staircase to the room where she slept with her brother. She had a small room of her own, but it was used more as a cupboard due to the dampness of its walls and its bitter cold in winter. The mumbled voices downstairs were too quiet to be truly calm. Mary began crying again as she pulled the ruined dress from her body and sat on her bed. She had disobeyed her mother. She had gone near the hot burn without an adult, and now she would never be forgiven. Perhaps her father would spank her with the heavy leather belt. She had disobeyed her parents, whom she loved, and that was why she cried.

She seemed to sit in her bedroom for a very long time, and she heard the front door opening and closing several times. She was trapped there. It was as if she had been told in school that someone was going to beat her, and having to go through the rest of the day in fear of the bell for going home. She stared at her dirty dress and sat and waited. Finally, a heavy noise on the stairs told her that her father was coming up. He opened the door and looked in on her. She was shivering, naked. He had the coal-dust still on him and his piece-bag slung over his shoulder. His eyes burned, but he came over and rubbed his daughter's hair. He asked if she was all right, and she nodded and sniffed.

'Let me get washed then,' he said, 'and we'll clean you up and get you dressed.'

There seemed a conspiracy in the house for the rest of the day, with no one mentioning what had happened. Her father washed her and helped her into her good dress and she sat by the fireside while he read a book. They were alone in the house. Much later, after her father had made some toast and jam and she had said that she was not hungry and still had not been scolded, the front door opened and closed quietly and Tom came in. He sat at the table with them and drank tea. Then Mary's mother came in, taking off her coat as she entered the living room.

'By God, I told them,' she said. Her face was flushed and her hands fluttered about her as she made a fresh pot of tea. 'I told them.'

When the family were seated around the table, they began to talk. It seemed that Mary's mother had gone round to Mr Duncan's house and Mr McLeod's house and had had words with each of them. Tom smiled twice as his mother told her story, but his father was quick to admonish him on both occasions.

Mary was made much of that evening, being allowed to stay up well past her bedtime. Neighbours came to sympathise and to find out just what Mrs Miller had done. These women sat with their arms folded tightly and listened carefully to their neighbour's narrative. They looked at the girl and smiled at her. By bedtime, Mary was aware that she was not to be scolded for her part in events. She went to bed with a lighter heart, but awoke twice during the night from a nightmare in which she was drowning again, but this time the faces above her were grim and unhelpful. An old man watched her and even seemed to be holding her below the surface, while a boy stood behind him and shouted. This boy looked quite like Tom, but was a bit older. She could not hear what he was shouting, but she saw him hammering on the old man's back. Then the hands of the goblins were upon her and she screamed through the water, waking up with her sheets knotted around her and her body drenched with sweat.

11

The following morning, Mrs Miller stared at the girl in horror. Mary's hair had turned silver in the night.

2

Her mother wrapped Mary's head in one of her own headscarves and walked with her down to the doctor's. It was raining, and a fine mist swirled around the large house which served Dr McNeill as both surgery and home. It was early still, but Mrs Miller made it clear to the housekeeper that this was an emergency. The housekeeper looked at the weeping, frightened child for a moment, then told them to wait in the hallway while she fetched the doctor from his breakfast.

Tears had made raw red streaks down Mary's cheeks. Her eyes were puffy and her face was confused. Her mother rubbed her shoulders, near to weeping herself. She tucked stray hairs back into the large headscarf and whispered what few words of comfort she was able to summon up from her common store.

Dr McNeill, white-haired and fifty, emerged at last from his dining room. He was buttoning his waist-coat, and had newly perched his half-moon glasses on his nose. Mary's mother apologised for interrupting him. He waved her apology aside.

'Well,' he said, patting Mary on the shoulder, 'and what seems to be the trouble here?' He knew the two of them very well, having treated Tom and Mary over the years for the usual run of childhood ailments. He knew that the mother was averse to seeing a doctor until the old cures, the myths and the herbs, had been tried and found wanting. So it had to be pretty serious for her to be here at this time of the morning, though things, it had to be admitted, did not *look* serious. 'I think we'd be better off in the surgery, don't you, Mrs Miller?' He guided them through the unfamiliar geography of his home until they reached the large room, full of cupboards, glass jars, table, chairs, and examining couch, where he held his surgeries. Usually you entered this room from the waiting room, which was itself reached via a door at the back of the house. Mary thought that the present journey was a bit like being an explorer, coming upon some welcome landmark. She was glad to sit on the familiar chair in front of the big desk. The smiling man with the scrubbed-looking hands sat across from her, and her mother sat nervously on a chair beside her. Her mother tugged gently at the headscarf, as if it were a bandage over a healing wound, and brought it clear of the girl's head. The doctor, coughing, came from behind his desk to examine Mary's hair. He stroked it gently while Mrs Miller explained about the incident of the previous day. He nodded and sighed several times before returning to his chair.

Mary's eyes had wandered by now, the adults seemingly intent in their conversation, and she studied the strange jars on the doctor's shelves. Some of them contained purple liquid and solid, jelly-like things. She would have liked to look at these things more closely, but a shiver held her back. Jelly was not her favourite dessert. One Saturday afternoon, while her mother had gone shopping along Kirkcaldy High Street, her father had taken Tom and her down to the beach. The sand was not white. Her father explained that it was all mixed up with coal-dust. By the water's edge were hundreds of washed-up jellyfish. Tom had prodded them with a stick, and sea-water had bubbled out of them. Mary had cried and her father had had to take her up to the promenade for an ice-cream, while, in the distance, Tom had explored with his stick the length of the tainted beach.

'Oh no,' the doctor was saying, 'no, it's by no means unheard of. You must know yourself, Mrs Miller, someone or other who has changed physically after having had a shock. Widows, people after a long illness, and others who have simply had a fright. Oh no, it's by no means unheard of, and I'm not one hundred per cent sure that the process is reversible. Mary's hair might remain like this for the rest of her days. She'll get used to it, of course, and so will her friends at school. I don't think there's any physical cause for concern. There might, however, be psychological damage, latent or otherwise. Time will tell, just as time will heal.'

The thing in the purple liquid looked as if it had drowned in that jar. Mary could imagine it twisting and pushing at the glass, but being unable to escape, rising to the surface to find that a lid was holding fast above it. No air, only an intake of purple water and the darkness, the goblins, the swathe of darkness, the choking in the throat and the final urge. The lid not budging.

Mary let out a scream.

She went to bed early and her mother wiped her brow, telling her to try to get some sleep. The light was left on in the bedroom. Neighbours were still dropping in to enquire about her, but they were kept downstairs, and though Mary leaned out of bed with her ear to the floor, still she could not make out much of the muted conversations. She felt like a leper. The quiet in and around the house was funereal, and Mary hoped that she would die soon. She tiptoed into her parents' bedroom and stole her mother's vanity mirror through to her own room. In bed again she examined her hair and saw how it aged her pale face, how it seemed someone else's hair, even when she pulled it. Not a girl's hair, but the hair of an old woman, a woman no one would ever marry.

When she heard her father's boots heavy on the stairs again, she hid the mirror under her pillow and lay down as if asleep. Her father entered the room quietly, his breathing desperately controlled, and touched ever so lightly her silvery hair. Mary jumped up and clung to him, the tears gurgling in her throat. He wept with her, sitting himself on the edge of the bed. 'Great God Almighty,' he said. 'Sshh, sshh.' He patted her softly, cradled her, and finally calmed her so that she was lying down again. He lay on his side beside her and told her that the

16

two big boys had got a hiding from their fathers, and had been hunted by her mother besides. He told her that one of them, Matty, would be starting work at the pit in a few weeks and would get a thumping from him at that time, just to let him know what was what. He told her a story about a princess with long silver hair and about the prince who saved her, but he stumbled as he spoke, and Mary could see that it was not a real story at all, but one that he was making up and that had never been true. Sometimes her father treated her as if she were still a little girl. She was ten, she often told him, and did not believe in made-up stories any more. Stories had to be true; stories had to be real. Her father's stories were those of a tiny child with a will to believe, and they seemed the only stories he had. He patted her hair again as if it were a kitten, then told her that she must try to get some sleep, for she would have to go to school tomorrow.

No, she thought when he had gone. She could not go back to school so soon. But it was true: the summer was already over. She would be ill. She would be ill until her hair turned black again. She could not go to school when she was so very ill. Her friends would visit her in her bedroom and would not comment upon her hair, because hair that colour suited someone so very ill.

When her mother wakened her with a shout next morning, Mary leapt out of bed and rubbed her eyes. She whistled as she dressed. Tom was still asleep, and she hit him with his own pillow, reminding him of the new term, and that he was starting at secondary school today and wasn't he excited? He groaned with his head beneath his pillow.

At the breakfast table her mother sat with a beautiful shawl around her shoulders. Mary sat down and took a bite from a slice of toast on her plate. Her mother smiled warily.

'How are you this morning, pet?' she said. Only then, in that scalding second, did Mary remember: the hot burn; her silver hair; her illness. She spat out the grey lumps of toast and ran upstairs to be sick.

3

Mary learned quickly the rules of the game. To defeat the disability she had first to ride with it and make a casual joke of it in company, never admitting the pain inside, turning it to her advantage. In this way, she soon found her friends to be much the same as ever, and discovered that people accepted her, though with pity.

There was still some suspicion, naturally, though few doubted the ability of a shock such as she had had to turn a person's hair white. Actually, some black did reappear in her hair. She became accustomed to brushing it in front of her new mirror. In a school full of nonentities, she found her identity easier to achieve than most. She was a kind of celebrity. Her mother did not take her back to see Dr McNeill and his purple jars.

Two weeks after school restarted, however, there was a horrible accident at the pit. Matty Duncan had been working there for a single day. On that first day he had been knocked almost unconscious by Mary's father. He had expected it, of course, and assumed that would be the end of it. He went to work on the second day with a careful smile on his shifting face.

19

He was a wage-earner now. His parents were pleased that some more money would be coming in, and Matty himself was only too glad to be out of school at long last and in his rightful place beside the other men of the village. He watched the wheel turning above the pit-cage as it creaked and brought the iron cage to the surface. He stepped in with the others and muttered the usual comments with them, careful to be respectful at all times. He descended into the scoured earth, slipping below ground level, deeper than the open-cast quarry, deeper, it seemed, than everything in the world. The descent took an age, the ropes creaking and shuddering. Matty thought of his first wages, and then, with a horrible opening of some door which he quickly closed, of the many days and weeks and years he could spend descending this shaft. A lifetime of burrowing, of coughing and spluttering and getting dead drunk on a Saturday. No, he thought, that's not for me. This was just pin money. When he had saved enough he would go to England, or even America. He would not be trapped into living an underground life like the poor buggers around him. First things first, though. Before he began saving he had to buy himself a record-player and a motorbike and get together some money for a holiday at Butlins with Tam Corrie.

The cage jolted to a stop. Someone pulled the gate back and they stepped out into the cold, dripping darkness. As he walked along the tunnel, Matty's head was full of other things he would do with his money. Cigarettes. Beer. No problem.

There was a rumbling from ahead. He peered in front of him, shining his torch along the tunnel. He moved to the front of the pack, showing his keenness. The others were mumbling.

'By Christ,' said one of them, 'that could be a cave-in up ahead.' They moved forwards a little, and the rumbling grew louder. Much louder.

'Get back to the fucking cage!'

They were running, and suddenly Matty was at the rear of a line that scurried too slowly towards the light at the end of the shaft. He could not get past the older, lumbering men. The bags over their shoulders slapped against the sides of the narrow passage. Great shadows were being cast everywhere, as if their pit-lamps were searchlights shining into the night sky. Then the light was brighter, a sudden eruption of daylight. Matty turned towards the rumbling and the fireball hit him full in the face and body, before flying up the shaft towards the ascending and empty cage.

They stood around the young man's body. Their backs and hair were singed, some badly, but the boy had taken the brunt of it. His whole front was black, charred as if he had spent an infernal lifetime digging coal. The smell of burnt flesh was overpowering. His hair was nothing, a few curled and brittle stalks. His face had melted back to the raw flesh. One man retched quietly in the corner while the cage descended and a crowd at the surface shouted anxiously through the smoke down the echoing shaft of sunlight.

*

'The boy saved my life,' said Mary's father later. 'I was right behind him when he fell. If it hadn't been him, it would have been me. I knocked him out one day, he saved my life the next. It doesn't seem right somehow.'

It was after Matty's death that the rumours began and Mary, who had survived a drowning and whose hair had turned silver overnight, found herself as marked by the accident as did the miners with their scorched backs and their memories of that hot, crisp smell.

4

Mary's hair turned no darker and no lighter. She grew up like her friends, and in five years seemed to have put the events of her childhood behind her. Her eyes took on glints of female knowledge and her speech modulated to the knowing tones of those who stood against the wall of the village café to discuss dating and pop music. Mary's hair was thick and long, and her eyebrows were as dark as her eyes. She had a sensual quality which many boys admired, and her boyfriends were many. Never did she think back to that night when she had told herself that no boy would ever look at her in her ugliness.

She did not really notice that Carsden was slowly fading in strength as she grew. It was the most insidious and subtle of changes, and she was not alone in ignoring the fact and its consequences. The miners were looking around them for other, productive pits. The mine at Carsden was proving difficult. The seams of coal were fragmented and thus hard to mine at a keen rate. Economics became a new word on the lips of the women shopping in the recently opened supermarket. This was 1968. Far away there was talk of revolution and radical change. The world was slipping and sliding on the edge of a new era of communication. Carsden slept longer and deeper than most. The houses were still furnished in the non-style of the late 1950s, and the men and women still wore the same period clothes. They talked about and thought the same things as they had always done. There was little place for discussion and change in a place which was concerned with survival at the most basic level. Soon, however, it became clear that the good days, such as they had been, were over, even for communities like Carsden who refused to accept that this was the case. The local colliery was mined out. Kaput. Nothing could be said which would have improved things, and nothing would have been said in any case, so nobody said anything. They just muttered under their breath conspiratorially, blaming everything that came to hand in cold, dull voices – everything except themselves.

The lie of the land was indeed the cause of it all, so the local paper said. The strata of rock around the village had been squeezed into awkward layers through the course of millennia, to the point where seams were narrow and often only ten or so feet long anyway. The National Coal Board said that coal was more expensive to mine in Carsden than its selling price per ton.

So people looked to the elements and cursed the economics which had robbed them of their livelihoods. Coal was the life force, the king of the land, and when the king died there was nothing left but the anarchic struggle to find new jobs, the rush to emigrate. And emigrate they did. Many of Carsden's younger inhabitants just packed up and moved the twelve or so miles that would ensure them a job in light engineering or electronics. The older ones, the unemployable ones, were left to watch the first wave of children move out. They had to realise that a bus ride would now separate them from their grandchildren. Drained of these lives, the old town became dry and cracked and hardened, its buildings seeming to frown at every passing car.

Moving, however, caused problems for the emigrants. They found it hard to make friends in the pioneer New Towns. They had been born in Carsden with their family around them like a tribe. They had been educated there, had met their friends at school there, had married there. Suddenly they were in strange territories, where the harling was white on the walls and the shopping centre was under cover and spacious and little factories opened up all around the houses offering work on production lines. There seemed no security in these kinds of job. These were ready-made societies all right, but they lacked the essential womb-like warmth which had been the mainstay of the old village. Suddenly neighbours did not know one another. There was room only for cold nods of the head in passing, and the occasional argument when a party or a television was too noisy. Still, the streets were relatively clean, and the facilities were good, if impersonal: created for rather than by the community.

And all this caring was in place of something opaque, intangible, something the migrant families knew they missed but were unable to express in words.

Soon a few of the earliest colonists had even straggled back to the village, to ponder the imponderable and wheel the baby's pram round to the parents' house again at weekends. They all had similar tales to tell of life outside Carsden: it was an unfriendly world. The furthest most of them ever travelled thereafter was to Blackpool in July.

Still, the trend was towards getting out, and if they could not get away for ever then they got away at weekends, visiting the same growth towns they had despised and spending their money on the week's food from the vast, spotless supermarkets. They bought knick-knacks from the large stores, and drank in pubs promising something better, more upmarket than those back home.

Buses departed on the hour to Kirkcaldy and Glenrothes, and Mary watched in fascination the sunken faces that rode the red vehicles towards the coast or the interior. Their eyes were pink and vacant, their skin sallow. The old ones wore cheap clothes and chatted mindlessly about the television and the neighbours. The young families snapped at each other like lions beneath a parched tree. The teenagers were dressed as the magazines told them to, but their hair was lank, slick. Their voices were loud as their eyes grinned at the pathos around them into which they were so keen to grow. They could be seen like this any Saturday, sitting with the rest in the tight seats, jerking whenever the driver changed gear.

This was the Carsden Mary inherited when she was fifteen and at the vital stage of growth. Her father sat in his chair much of the time. He had been made redundant a short time before and was bitter, cursing his inability to make manifest his innermost feelings. Mary's mother still crocheted shawls and clothes, and they still sold well. They were well made. But even she was suffering, was going blind slowly and making mistakes she would not have made five years before. Mary saw all this, but thought little of it. She was a teenager, and had to be out of the house straight after the evening meal in order to go down to the park for a smoke and a chat with some boys and friends of hers. If she had to go near the murky trickle of water that had once been the hot burn, she did so with scarcely a thought, laughing off any remembrance of the day. She would chat in the grocer's with the new Asian family, despite her father's protestations, and would buy sweets from Mr Patterson at the Soda Fountain, though there was a better selection at the supermarket. She made choices consciously now, for she was growing up.

And she was still close to her brother Tom, who was working in a light engineering firm in Glenrothes but stayed at home still, being just seventeen. She would be leaving school in nine months or so. The prospect excited her, though Tom shook his head when she enthused about it. He looked less cheerful now than when he had still been at school. A gradual process of disaffection had led him to argue a few times with his father. Mary did not usually understand the cause or substance of these fights, but would take Tom's side against the wheezing, ruddy-faced man anyway, and then feel guilty afterwards. Her father would be in a sullen mood for days, and she would make him cups of tea and try to smile him into cheerfulness. She thought that she might like to be a nurse one day.

She had a boyfriend too: a friend of Tom's, though a year younger than him. She was not sure that she liked the boy, but he was older than her so she persisted with him. He would talk with Tom about emigrating, and Tom would listen keenly. When Tom said one evening at the dinner table that he was emigrating to Canada, Mary ran upstairs and locked herself in the bathroom. Tom sat the whole evening at the kitchen table talking with his parents. His father brought out a bottle of whisky and two of the good glasses so that they could discuss things in the proper tones. Tom's mother was pale and silent. She studied her hands for most of the evening. The boy looked at her hands, hands capable of intricate weavings, and felt about to give in to their silent pressure. But this was not a decision that he had made easily. He had gone into it with various people, and had been in touch with an old family friend, Jimmy Gallacher, who worked in Canada and would put Tom up and see that he got a job in one of the sections of his own factory. A Scot, it was said, could always get a start in Canada. All Tom wanted now was the chance to try. He needed his parents' consent, though, or the leaving would be all the harder. His father conceded to most of his points, while Mary coughed out her sobs as she sat in the bathroom.

That night, when Tom finally went to bed, having made sure that Mary had her back to him before he changed into his pyjamas, the whole house felt as though it had gone through a death. The air was full of a choking intensity. There might have been a coffin on the table in the front room.

As soon as Mary heard the unmistakable creak of Tom's bed and the rustle of the sheets being pulled up to his chin, she turned and sat up.

'Are you really going, Tom?' His hands were confidently behind his head, supporting him on the pillows. He had the look of a person who needed to do no more thinking, the look of a person who would not allow himself to go to sleep for some considerable time.

'It looks like it. Will you miss me?'

'Oh, Tom,' she said, but could find nothing else to say, nothing that would have made any sense. It was a strange, tongue-tied feeling.

'Well, that's good,' he said. 'If I'm missed, it'll make trips home all the nicer, won't it?' He chuckled. Mary hurried from her bed and knelt on the cold linoleum at the side of her brother's bed. She was crying softly, the tears dredged up from some last ineffable source. His hands were in her hair, patting her, comforting her. He was struck dumb in a pleasing way. He had always been her big brother, but had never realised just what the bond entailed.

They sat together in silence for a time. Mary's

sobbing eased eventually, and a little later Tom thought that he had found some words for his little sister.

'We've all got to make this decision sooner or later, Mary. You'll have to make it yourself when you decide to leave home and get married or whatever.'

'I'll never leave here,' she said, her eyes searching his for some weak point. Tom shook his head.

'Come on,' he said. 'You're fifteen. You're not a baby any more. You'll want to leave soon enough when you see what it's like outside of school. Suddenly you're not special any more. Your friends have all gone off to become mature adults in boring jobs. You've not got enough brains to get a *really* good job, one that would take you away from the area. So what's left? The pits are closed. This town is becoming a dump. I'm not going to stay put in a dump. Not me. Maybe I'm not going to make anything of myself in Canada, but I'm not going to make anything of myself here either, so where's the difference?'

'But you've got us!' Mary whispered in anger and frustrated love. Tom was silent for a moment, his eyes forced finally to turn away from those of his fiery sister.

'Yes,' he said, 'but what happens when that's not enough? When that's not enough and I'm too old and weighed down to do anything about it? You won't always be here . . .'

'But I will, Tom, I will.'

'. . . and Mum and Dad haven't got more than ten

or twenty years left, have they? Everybody dies, Mary. It's the only fact of life.'

'You're sick!' she shouted. He shrugged his shoulders.

'Maybe I am,' he said, closing his eyes.

Mary ran to the window and stood there, her blurred eyes staring out on darkness. The night was still. She used to be able to see the winding-wheel at the colliery from this window, but now it had been dismantled. A good home had been found for it in a mining museum in the Lothians.

An old man was shuffling past uneasily below her. He stopped and leaned against the lamp-post, seemed to gasp for breath, then finally forced himself to move off again, his shoes dragging over the pavement. Tom was speaking behind her. He was approaching the window. She did not want him to look out. She turned and went to hug him, and there they stood, in an embrace of silent childishness, until Tom's feet got cold on the linoleum and he persuaded Mary to get back into bed.

5

It was a strange time, that autumn. Mary's father was drinking quite heavily, though her mother tried to hide the fact from everyone and succeeded only in hiding the truth from herself. Hugh Miller would sit in his chair until the early hours of the morning. Then he would say that he was going for a walk and would not be seen again until late evening, dead drunk usually and shouting along the length of the street about the treachery of the National Coal Board, the dirty tricks, the cruelty of it all. Mary, horrified and in her nightdress, would watch him from her bedroom window. She would watch her mother, hair falling to her waist in preparation for bed, having to leave the house and manoeuvre the roaring drunk around the lamp-post, which threw a garish orange glow over the proceedings, lending to them the hazy quality of something happening on a screen. Mary would watch them weave their way into the house, would hear her father retching into the toilet bowl or the sink. Tom would breathe heavily, pretending sleep, his pillow over his head. Mary was sure that he saw it merely as a ploy to stop him from leaving, and this seemed to make him all the more determined.

'What's the use?' her father cried. 'What's the use, eh? Where's the reason in it? They've shut the pits and they've shut this and they've shut that. What's a man supposed to do? No bloody use to anyone. That's me.' Mary's mother would whisper with patient vehemence at him, and having got him into bed at last, a basin at his side, would look in on Mary and Tom, both of whom would be lying in shade and in heavy silence, a lack of even breathing, which would confirm their mother's worst fears.

In the morning the pattern would be repeated. Mary grew sullen. A lot of things were to blame apart from her father's new-found dependence. Some of it had to do with a large prevailing mood in the town. Teenagers there had been brought up in the Sixties, had been told of the good life to come. Now, the Seventies approaching, they were being shown something else, and were seeing at last that behind every promise lay the bad news. There seemed nothing left to hope for. Everything was slipping further and further away. They talked about nothing else at school. Yes, they discussed jobs and career prospects, but behind it all was the greater knowledge that somehow the decline of the town was pulling them down with it, as if the town and its offspring were a single, inseparable unit.

And as they came to consciousness, so did Mary come into womanhood. She sat in her silent room after school, sometimes toying with homework but more often just staring at the walls and at the posters pinned there, posters of the pop groups who had come to represent the now untenable dream. She cried for no apparent reason. She began to have nightmares, the gist of which would be forgotten on waking. She saw the day near when Tom would be leaving: 6 January 1969. It was so close.

On Christmas morning Mary brushed out her long silver hair for some considerable time. She sat cross-legged on her bed with her mirror wedged in her lap, and watched the waves of static wafting strands around her as if she were sea-blown. A carol service was on the radio. Mary hummed along. She did not want to go downstairs because her father and mother would be there and last night her father had screamed at her mother and had slapped her. Mary had heard it through the bedroom floor. She could not face having to look at either of them or trying to speak to her father. Tom had been away all night at a friend's. He was home now. He was downstairs, where no one was speaking. The radio was loud in her room so that she would not hear the shouting, should there be any. This was the last Christmas before Tom left for Canada. She had looked at Canada in an atlas at school. It was huge, colossal really, and the towns and cities had good names. Some people there spoke French, but Tom could not. Why was he going to Canada when he could not speak French? It was far too late to put the point to him, so Mary brushed her hair and hummed carols instead.

Her mother shouted up the stairwell, her voice neutral. Lunch was ready. Mary felt as if she had just eaten a plateful of toast, yet she had to go down. There was no excuse.

She walked downstairs into silence. Her presents were the only ones left beneath the tree. Her father smoked in his chair. Tom, lying across the settee, was reading a book. Her mother could be heard singing softly in the kitchen. The large dining table had been ornately set. Mary drew out one of the chairs and sat down. There were six presents beneath the tree. There would be two from her mother and father, one from Tom, and three from her two aunts and one uncle. Her grandparents had died in the war. A whole generation had been erased.

Her mother brought in a steaming tureen of soup. 'Here we are then,' she said, and Mary thought that the smile on her bruised face was the saddest thing she had ever had to bear.

On Boxing Day, Mary's mother went to visit her sister in Leven, taking an overnight bag with her. Mary feigned illness and would not be persuaded to go. Tom had arranged to meet with some friends, as had Mary's father, so her mother left the house alone. The door clicked behind her. Mary did not expect to see her again. She saw it as her final leaving, and she did not blame her. When her mother returned the very next afternoon, no one but Mary was surprised.

But by then she was too distraught to be glad. Two months later, the family had their first letter from Tom in Canada, and Mary told her mother that she thought she was pregnant.

'Please don't tell Dad,' she said through her tears. Her mother remained silent for a long time.

'I'm not going to ask who it was,' she said eventually. 'Just answer me this: can he marry you?' Mary screwed up her eyes and shook her head. Her mother sat examining her own hands. It was not an easy life. First her husband had taken to drink, then she had to watch her only son leave for a distant country, and now this. Her son and her daughter. She knew immediately when it had happened. Boxing Day. The whole house had been changed somehow when she had walked into it on the afternoon following. She should have guessed. People had always said that they were very close, even for brother and sister. Unnaturally close. She should have known. She stroked her daughter's silvery dark hair and contemplated telling her husband the news. Would he guess what she had deduced?

As it turned out, Mary's father said nothing, just drifted further into his own numbed world where nothing, it seemed, could hurt him. Mary's mother was not surprised by this. She had always seen herself as the stronger of the two. He often called her 'the battler' (in the earlier years of their marriage at least) and she supposed it was true enough. Resilience, she had found, was needed in plenty. She went to church regularly, and knew that every trial was something more than it seemed – a higher test and a kind of judgement. She prayed to God at her bedside on the evening after she had told her husband the bitter news, and she made him get down on his knees too.

'This needs all our strength, Hugh,' she said, but his words were slurred and he collapsed his head on to the bed after a few moments and wept himself silently to sleep. Mary's mother raised her own head towards heaven and prayed with even more intensity. Strength was needed, Lord, strength was needed.

'But our reserves are not limitless, Lord. Help us in our need. Help Mary to get over all of this. She is a young girl. Forgive her if you can. Bless my son and my husband, Lord. Both are good men at heart. And dear Lord God, please let the baby die at birth. I beseech thee, let the baby die. Amen.'

6

If the unthinkable had happened, then for Mary's mother the worst had yet to come. For some time her husband had been friendly with George Patterson, a bachelor of forty who owned the town's dusty and outdated sweet shop. They often went further afield in their drinking bouts, travelling to Lochgelly or Kirkcaldy for an evening's entertainment and having to walk the sobering miles home after missing the last bus. In early April, with the town already knowing, as it inevitably would, that Mary was pregnant, and her mother stressing the need for her still to sit her exams, Hugh Miller was walking home with his friend George Patterson.

It was midnight, and enshrouded in a light mist the two men were unevenly trudging the grass verge towards Carsden. They had spent the evening in Kirkcaldy, and had gone down to the promenade after the pubs had closed in order to sniff the sea air. Hugh had sat on the sea-wall and had told George about the many occasions when he had walked with his children along the sands and bought them ices in the now defunct café. Having told his story, and having missed the last bus, they had begun to walk out of town along the main road. They tried hitchhiking, but were too drunk for anyone to have wished to stop for them, and both knew it. By midnight they were halfway between the two towns. They had become separated to the sight by the mist, but kept up a shouted conversation, the substance of which was lost to the wind and the bitter cold. A car came towards them from Kirkcaldy. Its lights caught George Patterson, and it slowed a little. He jumped from the road on to the verge and waved the car past. It was picking up speed again when George heard Hugh say something out loud and then there was a sickeningly dull and heavy thud. The car stopped. George Patterson could see its red tail-lights through the mist and ran towards them. At the side of the road lay his friend.

'For Christ's sake,' the driver was saying as he stood above the body in apparent horror. 'I mean, he just jumped out of nowhere. For Christ's sake.'

'Hugh, Hugh man, are you all right?' Patterson's breath was heavy as he crouched unsteadily beside his friend. Mary's father was able to raise his head a few inches from the frozen ground.

'I loved her, though, George,' he murmured, and then coughed a little and was dead.

For Mary's mother it was almost the end. The girl herself seemed almost too numbed by what had already occurred to be able to take in this latest tragedy, and her mother knew that Mary needed her strength. Indeed, it was that thought alone – that Mary needed her mother's strength – which kept Mrs Miller from plunging into madness and hysteria.

Instead she offered up increasingly bitter prayers to her Lord God and would receive mourners, many of whom were more interested in the condition of the daughter, with a smile like a bar of iron. Mother and daughter came closer and closer together during the arrangements for the funeral, the aftermath of the burial and the approaching birth. Tom could not be contacted, having apparently gone to the far north with a lumber squad, but Mrs Miller hoped that he would not come home in any case; not, at least, until the baby was born. She had forsaken her needle-work altogether, but would still make up one of her famed herbal remedies whenever anyone asked her to. Fewer and fewer people did. They had money enough to live on, she told Mary. Mary herself sat her exams, did poorly, but had her father's death taken into account come the final marking. She stayed at home all the time after that, and so was safe from the few wild and cruel rumours that flew around. Her father had committed suicide, it was said by some, and had done so because of the shame of his daughter's pregnancy. The lad – whoever he was – was to blame, said some, running away from his responsibilities. Then people remembered Matty Duncan, remembered the small witchy girl who had survived a drowning and who had sent a fireball on Matty to destroy him. Matty's father was the source of these new pieces of evidence. Mary was all bad luck, some agreed. But Matt Duncan shook his head. Luck did not enter into it. She had power: power over the elements, perhaps even power over her own brother and father. The bitter-cold mornings spent shopping in the town were enlivened by these increasingly speculative discussions, while all around Carsden was decaying and altering, as the boards went up across another shop's windows, wire mesh across the newsagent's, and the snooker hall closed down for ever.

Sandy was born in the middle of September. When she was released from hospital and was home, one of the first things Mary did was to take the tiny boy to his grandfather's still-fresh graveside in the town's cemetery. She held him in her arms and looked at the gravestone of shining grey and blue marble. Her mother stood beside her, a hand on her shoulder, and no tears were shed while the sun shone overhead and the baby lifted his face to the sky to gaze at the brightness. Crows chattered in the distance. The baby realised their presence and searched for a movement. He frowned when there was none. Afterwards, they walked back to the house in silence. The past had been somehow erased. The future could begin.

1985
Sandy

'One of those,' he said, and the man's plump hand fished in the glass jar for one.

'On the house, Sandy,' said the man, handing it to him and reaching over the crowded counter to ruffle the boy's unwilling hair. 'But don't tell your pals, mind, or they'll all be in here shouting about discrimination.' The man winked. 'And don't tell your mother. You know what she's like. I'm not giving you charity.'

Sandy smiled shyly. He was embarrassed by his standing as Mr Patterson's favourite. He knew that behind the action lay real pity for him. Mr Patterson was good that way; everyone said so. The old and the young women discussed him in the street with string bags full of shopping weighing from their arms like pendulums. They called Mr Patterson 'sweet' and 'a treasure'. Mr Patterson was a bachelor and owned the Soda Fountain, which was Carsden's sweet shop. He also cut hair in a tiny room at the back of the shop whenever anyone asked him to. He cut Sandy's hair sometimes, and would take great care when doing so. Sandy knew that Mr Patterson used to be friendly with his grandfather, and that Mr Patterson had been with his grandfather the night he had been knocked down. His mother had never spoken to him about that night, and so he assumed it was something nobody wanted reminding of. He knew that this was why Mr Patterson gave him his sweets free, and even money sometimes, especially at Christmas, but always with the admonition 'Don't tell your mother. You know what she's like.' Yes, Sandy knew. Mr Patterson's kindness would only remind her of times which had been pushed into the past in order to be forgotten. Sandy smiled, thanking Mr Patterson for the sweets.

'Cheerio, son,' said Mr Patterson, who was rubbing his pudgy hands together as if trying to wash away the stickiness of the sweets.

When Sandy left the shop its bell tinkled and some women outside stopped talking and stared at him instead. As he passed the silent huddle, sucking on the hard nougat, he wondered if they had been talking about his mother, and his face flushed. They would not be as generous as Mr Patterson in their words. Sandy was the son of the local witch, and although he seemed a nice enough lad – quiet, kind, polite – still you could never be sure. They pitied him his fate, whatever that might be, but they scrubbed at his clothes with their eyes, imagining the filth beneath.

Sandy could have told them that, being fifteen, he took baths often. He could have told them that the reason they thought him just a little grubby was his root-black hair, shot through with hints of blue. He had dark eyes too, with thick eyelashes which curled like a girl's.

It wasn't his fault if he was dark.

His mother's hair was silver and black, but mostly silver. It straggled down her back when she brushed it out in front of her mirror. His mother had dark eyelashes like his. Her face was pale and fragile. Yet the townspeople thought of her as the witchy woman, and she had never, to his knowledge, denied it. But she wasn't a witch, he knew as he swung his satchel to and fro and made his way vaguely homewards. She wasn't a witch.

It had begun even before he had started school. He had not wondered at his lack of friends. In his solitude it seemed to him that everyone had to be the same. Then the taunts had begun. Witchy, witchy, tinker, your mummy is a stinker, she casts a spell and runs like hell, witchy, witchy, tinker. And he a tiny boy and amazed by it all, carrying bread home to his mother and his grandmother. Witch. Tinker. If he came into the house with mud all over him from having fallen, then his grandmother would slap the front of her apron and stand back to mock him: 'Well, well,' she would say, 'and who's this wee tinker-boy, eh?' Tinkers were gypsies. They travelled around in cars and caravans and hoarded their money while pretending poverty. They came to your door and offered to sharpen your cutlery, then ran away with your forks and knives and sold them elsewhere. They tried to sell you flowers which they had picked from dead people's graves. They were dirty and sly and not to be trusted.

'I'm not a witchy-tinker!' he had shouted at the

pack of taunters one day. They had stood back a few paces at that, as if expecting him to lash out at them. His face was red. He repeated the denial and some of them giggled. He started to chase them, but they flew apart like leaves in a sudden breeze. He touched one or two, no more. They shrieked and ducked and flew further from his reach.

'I've got bugs!' one yelled. 'The tinker got me!' The others had laughed and he had continued to chase them. The boy who had cried out stood catching his breath and trying to blow on to the spot where Sandy had touched him, as if that would cleanse the stain. Sandy walked up to him, the loaf of bread squashed beneath his arm, and touched him again. The boy screeched. Someone said, 'You're it!' and the boy began to chase them all. Sandy soon caught on and ran with the best of them, dodging and weaving and never once being touched. His grandmother called to him from the end of the road. Everybody stopped playing and looked towards her.

'Come on, Sandy. Tea's ready.' He began to walk away.

'Cheerio,' said one of the girls.

'Aye, I'll see you.' Sandy began to trot towards his retreating grandmother. He was eager to tell his mother that he had been playing with his friends.

Was it soon after that that his grandmother had died? He could not remember exactly. No, it was after that that she had taken the first of her bad turns; the first at which he had been present. It had scared him for days afterwards.

He had described it to his new friends as they

played behind the picture-house. 'She couldn't speak or anything,' he had told them. 'She just sat in her chair. Her mouth was open a little and she was dribbling. Spit was running down her jersey.' They made funny faces at that. One or two laughed. The girls seemed more intrigued than the boys. 'And her hand was shaking like somebody shivering, but she was sweating. She was like that for ages. Sometimes her eyes would open. Then they would close again.' The girls gasped in horror at the thought.

'Sounds like what happened to my uncle,' said one of the boys, chalking his name on the wall with a stone. 'He was sitting reading in the house one day and the next thing he was on the floor. He coughed and blood came out of his mouth.' He gazed at them to fathom the effect of his words. One of the girls put her hand to her throat and said, 'Eeyuk,' while another closed her eyes and clamped her hands over her ears theatrically. Even Sandy was sweating a little as he imagined the scene. Blood coming out of your mouth! It was horrific. He tapped his fingers on the stone wall and tried not to look a sissy. He noticed that the other boys were doing much the same thing. Someone suggested a game of football and it seemed like a good idea, but the ball was at the boy's house in Dundell, and Sandy didn't think he was allowed to go that far away. He watched them all leave, still shouting at him to join them. He smiled and shook his head.

'I'm going somewhere with my mum,' he lied. 'I think we're going to Edinburgh.' He flushed immediately, ashamed of the whopper. He walked home slowly, kicking a stone the length of Main Street without it once rolling on to the road. He left the stone outside his gate and went indoors. It was a good stone, and he would keep it. By the following morning he had forgotten it, and when he finally did remember a few days after that the stone had disappeared. He found another, better one, and thus had started his collection of good stones.

He thought about his mother's hair now as he walked up the street from the Soda Fountain. Black and silver, hanging in thick threads. Black night shot through with wisps of moonlight. He had described it like that in one of his English essays. He liked English, and especially liked writing essays. He got good marks for them. He had been rather annoyed when his mother had started going out with his English teacher, Mr Wallace. Now people would think that any future good marks were due to that and not because he was good at writing things. He had seen Mr Wallace stroke his mother's hair as if checking that it were real.

'Don't pull them out,' his mother used to say if Sandy's curious fingers lingered over the silvery threads. 'They just come back in thicker than ever.' When she had said that he had thought that maybe she was a witch after all. She was something magical that talked on bad days with the long dead and sang sacred songs with a shawl strewn over her lap in the small back room where the memories were kept. Some warm Sundays, if he was in his bedroom with the door a little ajar, doing his homework, he would hear her voice lullabying spirits in that back room. Her hair would be hanging around her in a manner that caused Sandy to stir uneasily in his adolescent body. He would chew on his ballpoint pen and stare at the wall. There were no exams important enough to be worth studying for on days like that, days which would be emerging again soon by the look of the buds on the trees, though there was a coolness to the sun still, like porridge watered and milk-soft.

He clambered over a wall and skirted the edge of a field. His mother would be expecting him home, but she was not anxious these days if he was a bit late. He was fifteen and could stay out till after ten o'clock if he liked; could say that he had been visiting a friend without really having to lie. He had some friends at school – Mark, Clark, Colin – but he could not visit them comfortably in their homes. Sometimes they flushed as they tried to lie an explanation to him as to why he could not actually enter their houses. He was old enough now to shrug off most of the resentment. He knew that it was the old-fashioned stubbornness of the parents that was to blame, that kept him waiting at street corners, hands slouched low in his pockets. He knew that some of his friends even had to lie to their parents in order to go out with him. Fuck that. Fuck that. Could he dye his hair and change his mother into something else? That was it all right. That was it. His shoes stamped deeper into the soft earth as he trudged towards his destination. At least he could be sure of being accepted there without fear of embarrassment. Even if it was dangerous. Even if someone saw him and

51

told his mother. Did anyone care about him that much or mind him that much? He doubted it.

On the golf course to his left some men were shouting and hitting the ball off the first tee with a satisfying swish. Sandy might want some clubs for his birthday in September, a whole summer away. If he had a job he could save the money to buy them. He had only to wait until Christmas. He could not leave school until Christmas. Then he would buy everything on his list: golf clubs and motorbike and all. He would get a job in Glenrothes if he could, and one day he might move away from the area. His mother wanted him to stay on at school to do Higher exams. Where was the future in that? The only future was to see yourself at the first tee with your half-set or even full set of clubs, plus all the extras. Teeing off, the ball going swish into the sky like a tiny satellite. That was the future. He climbed another wall, higher than the first, and was in the garden of an empty mansion.

2

Her grandmother had made the most beautiful shawls, crocheted intricacies of nature. She placed them back in the chest. Her mother too had worked with wool. A jersey remained, as fresh as washing on a line. She put it back, patting it neatly into place on top of the shawls. There was still a good six inches of space to the brim of the chest. She could not hope to fill that space, for her own hands were out of touch with delicacy. They could never know the peace of mind that comes with patterns. She closed the heavy lid of the brass chest and sat down on it, humming softly. This room smelled damp even in the spring and summer. In winter it was an ice-box, unusable. No electric fire could take anything but a superficial chill from the air, leaving still the depth of the room's iciness, a depth beyond mere physical presence. She looked at her watch. He would be home from school soon, her son, her only child, her bastard. Born out of shame . . . But what was the use in thinking about all that? She had spent too long thinking back to it. She rose from the chest and started downstairs, holding on to the banister with one of her long, awkward hands. She felt weak today. Her period was coming on. She would have to be careful not to snap at Sandy. He was always in a sulk these days. His age, she supposed. He was either out for much of the night, or else sat in his room with the record-player blaring, and even when he deigned to slip downstairs around ten o'clock he would say that he had been studying. What could she say to him? She fingered her silver-dark hair. If only her mother were here; she could talk to him, and he would listen. She had held him spellbound with her long, rambling stories right up until the day before she had died. Sandy had cried at his grannie's funeral. Would he cry at hers? Oh, of course he would. She was being stupid again.

She began to check the pots on the cooker, stirred one of them and replaced its lid. Everything was fine, but where was he? It looked as if he was going to be late again. She sighed, but set the table anyway, making sure to put out the tomato pickle to which he had so taken recently. She had found a recipe for it in one of her magazines and would make some of her own soon. She sat at the table and let her fingers dance over the cloth. Dance to your daddy, my little laddie. She felt most comfortable late in the evening when, Sandy in bed reading and the lights out and the fire still glowing brightly, she would speak to her mother and sometimes even her father. There was comfort in speaking to the dead, and it showed that you had not forgotten them. How could people forget their dead? Yet they seemed to. After a while, the funeral a few weeks past, they would just stop talking about them, and all the traces of grieving would leave their faces so that the living could begin again in earnest. That was unwise. She knew that that was unwise. You had to keep their memory burning brightly and then they did not really die, then you could speak to them at their graveside or in your own living room. You had, in effect, lost nothing.

He's too late now. He's not coming. Probably he's down at the corner with his friends and the girls who hang around with them. He still blushed when she mentioned the possibility of there being a special girl in his life. He still shook his head. He was a fine-looking boy. He would not stay innocent for much longer. Fifteen. Fifteen. That's how old she had been . . . But what's the use? No bloody use at all. Here she was, nearly thirty-two, having done nothing with her life other than bring up Sandy. She knew that she could not put into words how important that made him to her. He was everything, and she thanked God that the townspeople had taken to him at last and let him become one of them. She had always resented their shunning her. She still felt bitter sometimes. The years had been hard. They could have been harder, yes, but they would have been a lot easier had she been accepted and not made subject to stupid rumours about witchcraft and the like. She felt like sticking pins in the whole lot of them. If only they would accept her, or even cast her out altogether. But no, instead there were the looks and whispers, the snide jokes. They would go no further. If she pressed them, they would tell her that they were merely having a bit of fun, no harm meant. They were cowards; neither cold nor hot.

She found them despicable, and yet this was still her town, and these were still her people. Some of them were reasonable people, of course. The minister was very nice, and Andy made all the difference. Would he visit her this evening? She could not remember having arranged anything, but he might turn up anyway. Her stomach began to growl.

She sat at the table and ate her meal in silence. She heaped food on to Sandy's plate, covered it, and placed it in the warm oven. She then washed and dried the dishes, pots and utensils before making herself some coffee and taking it through to the living room. She looked out of the window for a while, then closed the curtains and switched on the television. She stood in front of the television and sipped her coffee. Eventually she sat in her chair, sighing once before doing so. She resigned herself to sitting like this for several hours. It was a dour prospect. On the screen a quiz show was reaching its climax. A couple from the west coast were dressed up in rabbit costumes and acting out a kind of pantomime. She thought of them sitting at home watching themselves and feeling embarrassed, but laughing it off because they had won the tea service and the grandfather clock and the decanter with six crystal glasses. These prizes would be crammed into their already overflowing house, and if they had video-recorded their efforts they would inevitably show it to any visitor from now until New Year. They would show off the decanter on a shelf in their wall unit. They would open a cupboard, and there, in shadowy hibernation, would be the tea service, awaiting that elusive 'special occasion'. They would squeeze past the dully ticking grandfather clock in their narrow hall when they went to bed at night. Their life had been full. Mary wondered why she watched these programmes at all. They did not excite her. People shopping on the following morning would talk about the television programmes, would mention the prizes on the quiz shows admiringly. They seemed excited by it all. Real people, she supposed, were being shown winning for a change, but it was a hollow enough victory.

There was a knock at the door: one, two, three in rapid succession – Andy. She flicked channels to a documentary, and examined herself in the mirror. It was far too late to do anything about her appearance. She hurried to the door and opened it. The street lamp was on now, though the sky was still blue, a deepening blue as if it were a sea rather than a sky. Andy was smiling.

'Sorry for interrupting,' he said, but she was already ushering him awkwardly inside. 'And so late. I hope I'm not . . .'

'Nonsense, Andy. I was going out of my mind. Yet another quiet night in front of the goggle-box.' She felt more relaxed once the door was closed, separating them from the outside world of looks and whispers, whispers and looks. She could feel him relax too. 'Sandy didn't come home this evening, so I've not spoken to a soul all day.' This was a white lie. She had spoken to the usual people whom she met while shopping. She had also spoken to her mother, who would turn in her grave if she heard her daughter lying. Mary giggled to think of it, and Andy continued to smile.

'Anything good on the box?' he asked, still a slight distance from her.

'No,' she answered, nearing him and hugging his waist. 'We'll switch it off.' Their lips touched.

They had met at a parents' night. She had spent an age that evening in her bedroom making herself presentable. She always liked the teachers to know that Sandy's mother was nicer than local folklore would have them believe. Mr Wallace was quite new to the school then, and quite new to the area. An outsider, she had thought, a bit like herself. They had got on famously. It had been a few weeks later, however, when they had bumped into each other in Kirkcaldy, that he had actually asked her if they might go for a drink some evening. She had asked him if that were not rather irregular, having already decided to go. He had mumbled something flattering. Yes, it was that meeting that stayed in her mind rather than the more formal first encounter. She had wondered at the time about the propriety of the thing, but Sandy had not batted an eyelid on discovering their attachment. Word spread like wildfire, of course, and the town saw it as a bewitchment. She had made a schoolteacher break the silent golden rule. Andy's headmaster had spoken to him twice about it, but as yet the young man was refusing to give in to any discreet pressure. He still saw the mother and he still taught the son, and the town still whispered with hissing venom behind their backs. Carsden had become just a little colder since then, but Andy did not care. He knew that he was infatuated, and he knew that the infatuation was worth anything, even if it meant having to resign. Sometimes he wondered if the woman with the old hair and young face, who could tell so many bitter tales, really was a witch. Sometimes there seemed no other explanation. Then he would become rational again and smile at his foolishness. Just as he was smiling now, sitting with a cup of coffee in one hand while the other curved against Mary's back. The radio playing old songs. The newly kindled fire sparking its way into life.

'I had a letter from my brother this morning,' Mary said. 'He's very interested in you. He likes to take an interest in what's going on.'

'He's never been back here, has he?' asked Andy, pushing gently at the tight contours of her spine.

'Not for a long time,' she said.

3

Weeds sprouted regally through the growing mesh of lawn around the mansion. They crept, too, along and up the cracked and flaking walls. Silent, insidious, they coloured the air with an aroma of rank and abundant decay, and tinted the house with the hue of disuse.

The mansion was silent beneath their onslaught, like an exhausted and dying elephant, once majestic. Its large ground-floor windows were securely covered by sections of wood which had dried and moistened through recurring seasons, twisting and knotting their sinews like those of a living thing. The upper floor, with its slightly smaller windows, had shutters too, but parts of these had slipped and fallen, allowing areas of glass to appear as targets for an evening's energetic and restless children. These jagged edges of glass caught the red of the early evening sun and seemed to run rust-coloured streaks to the wood beneath them.

People usually averted their eyes from this building whenever they passed, for they felt chilled by the boarded-up windows, by the complacent and public display of what was, after all, a slow death. The grand illusion of ownership.

The mansion, built in the late nineteenth century at the request of, it was said, a close friend of the Earl of Wemyss, was best known for the role it had played of hospital. No local knew its complete history, but it was known that it had once been Fife's first hospital for the treatment of tuberculosis, and many patients had entered through its doors for the promised revolutionary treatments. Its wards had quickly filled with those admitted by the local doctor and those from further away who hid in small private rooms and were visited daily by well-dressed people burdened with flowers and boxes of delicate chocolates. Curiously, the patients themselves all looked the same: the same pallid faces and heavy chests, the same defeated eyes. They would sit all day in front of the large windows and soak up what sunshine there was. This was in the early 1900s. Later, with tuberculosis a menace of the past, the hospital became a home for shell-shocked war veterans. Cries could be heard over the growing hamlet, the cries of men for whom war was still a raging demand on their nightmares. Later still, the local doctor moved into the sprawling house, but, finding it ghost-ridden and difficult to heat, soon moved out and into a smaller house which had once belonged to one of the local pit managers. People knew even then, in the 1960s, that the town was in some way preparing for its last stand, and the mansion became a symbol of incipient decay and neglect. No one, it seemed, wanted a ghostly house, a large damp house, a rambling hospital which had once been splashed with blood and bile and the echoing groans of madness and death. So it was that, after countless raids by gangs of children, the edifice was nailed shut. A local solicitor still held details of its owner and value, should any offer be forthcoming, but that was just so much dust and fawn-edged paper in some long-forgotten file. Much of the lead now gone from the roof, tarpaulin and polythene having taken its place, the mansion was a soiled relic, a fitting beast to be overlooking the smoky town from its slight and now anachronistic prominence, its quarter-mile of distance.

But home still to some.

Home almost to Sandy, who kicked at the pale yellow heads of the weeds as he crossed the raging lawn, scraping mud from his shoes on to the grass, hacking out the roots of purple-headed thistles with the heel of his left foot. He aimed at a dandelion and it swirled into nothingness with a feathery puff, its seeds scattering on the air towards the house itself. Sandy felt one strand tickling his nose. He sneezed and wiped his nose against the sleeve of his jersey, having pulled the arm down past the cuff of his jacket. 'God bless,' he said to himself. He made his way around to the back of the house. From here he could see across the low wall to the golf course and the countryside beyond. Very occasionally there was money to be made in the summer by caddying for those golfers who wanted their friends to see how affluent they were. He would have to keep that in mind now that the warmer weather was bringing those types out of hibernation. The only figures he could see on the course at present were already walking away from the first tee, and so had their backs to him. He clasped his hands around the drainpipe, tested it for the strain, and began to climb, his shoes scraping hard at the wall for support, kicking off tiny chippings of plaster, exposing even more of the brickwork beneath. His cheek grazed the rusting drainpipe. It was cold and ragged. When he looked up, the sun tried to blind him by flashing its light on to the shards of the window above. Not far to go now, though.

The first time he had climbed this drainpipe he had been petrified, had needed a push from below and the hissed advice not to look down. That had been when the house was a haven for children. They had wandered its corridors, let loose in an adult and sacred environment. They had made play of its rooms and its staircase. Now Sandy climbed quickly and skilfully, his legs sliding behind him as he moved in peristalsis towards the window ledge. That was always the most difficult part: at the top he had to swing towards the sill. His eyes would be catching side-swipes of countryside and he could feel the space beneath him trying to pull him down. His hand would rake across the sill, pushing at the wooden board until it fell back with a clatter into the dusty gloom of the house. The slight smell of mould caught his throat then, and made his heart beat a little more strongly. The feet swung out, caught the sill, hung over it, one hand still grasping the drainpipe while the other gripped the window frame. Then he had to release his hold on the pipe and heave himself inside. For a second he would be hanging back into space, his legs threatening to weaken as they tightened on the sill. Fear as much as anything drove his slow body through those few final inches. His arms ached from overuse, but he was safe. Looking out he saw only the vertical drop which would once have made him dizzy. He replaced the wooden board and was suddenly in a deep, shadowy half-light.

He was in a large room which would once have been a ward. The floorboards creaked from his unusual pressure upon them. The walls were grey-green, histories almost in themselves. The door was closed. He held his breath a little and turned the handle, then opened the door quickly in order to have it over and done with. He was in an empty corridor. The windows along its length threw substantial shadows across his path. He walked uneasily along the corridor, past several open doors which, thankfully, let him peer into their dull interiors to assure him that nothing was there. He found himself, in the end, confronted by a closed door which had to be opened if he was to continue. By now, though, it was more a game than anything else. No surprises had been planned today, and he could relax. He opened the door easily, just as he would have the living-room door at home, and walked into a room which contained two dark figures who shuffled away from him.

Sandy smiled at them. The man came forward and ruffled his hair.

'And how are you, Sandy boy?' His voice was clear and deep. It might have been Irish, sounding as if it had been arranged specially for the occasion, as one would have arranged a room in which to receive visitors. Smooth as a velvet dress, it faded behind him as its owner left the room: 'Just going to take a leak.' The door was pulled shut until only a gash of crimson light was left to lend any reality to the scene.

There she was, though, crouching low by the fireplace, her arms stretching down to the floor as she balanced herself on her toes. She felt comfortable like that, she had told him. She was a black cat about to strike. Sandy smiled towards her blurred face, etching her with an inner eye before approaching. He squatted down near her.

'Hello, Rian,' he said. She brushed her hair away from where it lay across her solemn face. Her eyes seemed to cut through the space between them like metal through water. He was, as always, affected by her, and he coughed his nervous little cough and bowed his head to a meditative silence. Bugger you, he thought. I'll not speak again till you do. They sat and awaited the brother's return. Sandy was about to speak when the door opened behind him.

'Hands off, Sandy. That's my bloody sister that you're manhandling there.' He adjusted his crotch as he entered, as though he really had been urinating. Sandy smiled and the young man chuckled. 'I know you young lads,' he continued, 'and you're all after just one thing. You won't let up until you get it. Well not from my sister you don't.' He chuckled again and Sandy smiled compliantly. The man was glancing nervously towards the girl. Sandy knew that for all his bravado, all the shoulder-punching and joking, Robbie really feared the girl. It was the fear that he would go too far in his jokes, in his teasing, the fear that she was more than she seemed. It appeared to Sandy that this somehow gave *him* an amount of power over the brother. He could sit in silent naivety and wait. Wait for all time. His eyes now sought those of the girl, but they were not yet to be had.

Robbie lit a candle between them, kneeling so as to make a triangle of crouched figures.

'That's better,' he said. 'It's definitely getting lighter these evenings, though, Sandy.' The boy nodded. Robbie, for all his ways, was only five or so years older than him. His growth of beard was thin and slow, and his eyes were playful and filled with a bright life still to be lived. Yet he was his sister's protector, and so was a man. He had been a man almost from the day Rian had been born. His aunt had provided the feeding of the pair of them, it was true, but the small boy who had watched his mother's newly dead face being covered with a lace handkerchief and who had touched her cold forehead while simultaneously hearing the mewling of the new-born baby had known at once that he had somehow become his own father, though he could not be allowed to run away as his father had done so bitterly. His sister and he were inextricably joined by thick blood, and he would be a little soldier, as his Aunt Kitty repeatedly told him to be, and fend for his sister until the time came for an adult parting. Thereafter he had held tiny, rubber-bodied Rian in his arms as gingerly as if she had been a good china

66

plate. He had watched her sup on her bottle, had tipped her over his shoulder and rubbed her soothingly, coaxing her to laugh, which she seldom had done. Sometimes, however, she had managed a little soldier's smile back at her brother.

'I was a father at six,' his story to Sandy had begun, 'and to this little horror at that!' His thumb had jerked towards the faintly smiling girl. She had been curled on a blanket like a small kitten, Sandy recalled, and had sucked the edge of the blanket as though she were still teething. She had smiled that first time, but had said little. He had forced his eyes to remain trained on Robbie's face, not wishing him to perceive his own interest in the girl. Only when she had spoken had he turned to her, drawing in huge gulps of her as if she were water to his thirst.

He had fallen in love on that first day, and had known it, for he had thought about her all the next week at school and had walked often past the mansion hoping for a glimpse of her. On the following Friday, as had been agreed on that first day, after that surprise meeting (he had expected to find nothing but ghosts and memories in the old hospital), he had returned to the room. Robbie, drinking from a beer can and smoking a cigarette, had noted Sandy's acute embarrassment at even being in the same room as her. He had leaned across to the boy and given him a stinging slap on the thigh, saying, 'Ah, Sandy, Sandy, so you've caught the fever, eh? Too bad, son, too bad. It happens to the strongest men when they look at Rian, when they see that shining innocence, that knowing look, that mystery.' He had risen to his feet. His eyes were on his sister as she sat on her blanket. He had staggered a little, dragging his feet around the room while the candle sent grotesque shadows dancing on the walls. 'Me too, man. Me too. She caught me before anyone else, before she could walk even, and only the thought of my . . .' he struggled with language, the mystery of words he needed but did not know, and frowned '. . . my task, or something – only that knowledge, and the drink of course, keep me from . . . keep me sane.' He had leaned over his sister, studying her face as if he were a painter, his words hanging in the smoky air. Sandy had thought it time he was going. His cheeks were burning. He was full of questions and emotions. Robbie had slid silently down the wall and rested his chin on his chest. She had risen, had seen him silently to the window, had allowed him out on to his ledge before reaching forward to kiss him on the cheek. Still her face had remained a mask. She might have been kissing the minister. He slipped down the pipe uneasily. His heart had been trembling. It would tremble for a long time as the kiss grew in his fertile mind.

That had been a full month ago. Now Robbie looked on Sandy as part of the scenario, albeit a moving, trustless part; the kind of thing a gypsy could appreciate.

'What's it like being a gypsy?' had been Sandy's first question to Rian. She had shrugged her shoulders. Robbie had answered for her.

'If gypsies are outcasts from their own tribe, then they're shadows in the dark, which is to say useless.'

Sandy knew that there was a loneliness in Robbie, and he could feel his visits bolstering the young man's sense of purpose. They were friends of a sort now. Rian was not Sandy's friend, nor could she be. A larger intent lay behind their thin but strengthening bond. It was something Robbie might one day find himself unable to stop. Sandy knew that his relationship with Rian would work inversely to his relationship with Robbie, and these were knotted strings with which his nimble fingers but clumsy brain played. Something was unfolding, and Sandy shut from his mind the notion that its culmination would be pain or despair or frustration. He simply refused to consider those possibilities. But he knew. And Robbie knew also, so that there was an inevitable tension in his visits: psychological jousting, with Rian looking on as impassively as a fair princess. There would be no favourites in the game. Not yet.

Tonight Robbie was speaking about some of the day's incidents. Rian had been begging in Craigore, a nearby town. They had some cheese and bread if Sandy was hungry, and a little milk besides. 'Time was,' Robbie was saying, 'you could have gone down to the river and used the water straight from it for a pot of tea, but not now. Pollution. A gypsy used to fend well for himself before all this . . . this . . . plastic shit.' Sandy studied the beer can in Robbie's hand as he waved it around. He felt that Robbie's drinking was frowned upon by Rian. It might prove a useful weapon in the fight. He had not accepted a drink from Robbie yet, though he was keen to, for it was something that had to be done at his age. He had resisted in order to impress Rian, and she looked across at him whenever he denied himself as though she were unusually full of curiosity about him. 'Suit yourself,' Robbie would say, and would then finish the contents of the tin quickly and noisily, smacking his lips in challenging satisfaction afterwards. Tonight Sandy felt like saying: 'Always enough money for drink, though, eh Robbie?' That would have scored points, but it seemed unnecessarily cruel. Sandy said nothing; only listened and hoped that his princess would speak. Robbie talked about the snooker hall in Craigore. 'You can sometimes make a few bob on a game, but not often and never much money. They're tight-fisted in that town all right. Mean shower. Rotten snooker players too. Almost embarrassing.' He looked at Rian, then at Sandy, and crushed the thin beer can with one hand, rubbing at his nose with the other.

'An itchy nose,' said Sandy. 'My mum says that means you're going to come into money.' Having said it, he felt stupid. It seemed banal. Robbie's eyes lit up, however, and he shook his head vigorously.

'Your mum's wrong. An itchy palm means money. An itchy nose doesn't mean anything. No, wait a minute. That's not right. It *does* mean something but I just can't think what.' He furrowed his brow, put a hand across his eyes like a mind-reader. 'My Aunt Kitty used to tell me about all that stuff when I was a kid, but I've forgotten most of it. Superstitious crap.

No,' he shook his head and waved his hands in the air, 'I've forgotten it. She could help, though. My Aunt Kitty at the caravan.'

'Caravan?' said Sandy.

'Caravan,' said Robbie. 'Where the hell did you think we came from? We didn't just appear out of thin air, man. Didn't I tell you? Didn't Rian? We belong to the tinkers' site at the foot of Craigie Hill.'

'Then why did you move here?' Robbie hesitated at Sandy's question. He looked over to his sister, then at Sandy. Sandy nodded, though he felt that he had only half the picture. 'Oh,' he said.

'Yes,' Robbie continued, 'we should visit my Aunt Kitty some day.' He again looked to Rian, who suddenly came alive.

'She's *my* aunt too! She's not just *your* aunt!' She stared at her brother in a rage while he scratched his beard, then she blushed and dropped her eyes. Robbie chuckled.

'Oh?' he said. 'Well, maybe that's something to ask *her*, after what happened. Maybe all three of us should go up there just now and see what Aunt Kitty says to it. I seem to remember her saying something like "She's no relation of mine." Isn't that right then, Rian?' The girl was already on her feet. She moved swiftly, and in her movement Sandy was attracted to the shape of her body. She slammed the door as best she could behind her. Robbie hooted loudly, smiled at Sandy, then turned his eyes to the floor and thought to himself.

'I suppose I should be going,' said Sandy.

71

'But you've only just got here!' complained Robbie, who seemed genuinely upset.

'Yes, but my mum will have my tea ready. I'm hellish late for that.' Sandy had a sudden inspiration. 'And I want to ask her about the itchy nose. Then we can go and see your auntie. Okay?' For a second Sandy thought that it might have been a mistake to mention this, but Robbie nodded.

'Yes,' he said. 'You do that. Will you come back tomorrow?'

'Maybe, Robbie.' Sandy was already on his feet.

'Fine then.'

There was no sign of Rian in the corridor. 'Cheerio, Sandy,' said Robbie. As the door closed on him, he was hunting in his pockets for a cigarette.

'Cheerio, Robbie.'

He sat on the window ledge for a long time. Rian did not appear. Robbie was whistling in the far room. Sandy did not want Robbie to come out and find him still sitting there. It would be too much of an admission of interest in Rian. He sat for a full count of sixty. The golfers had abandoned the course. It was too dark now to play, though there was still a faint red glow in the sky. He reached out for the drainpipe and shimmied down, jumping the last five feet and feeling the drop through space thrill in his stomach. He landed with a grunt on the lawn. Some jotters had fallen from his satchel. He crouched and replaced them. When he stood up, she said something behind him.

'Don't believe him, Sandy. Don't believe anything he says. There's a streak of badness in him.' Her voice was quiet and sugary. He turned to her and she stepped towards him. It was the easiest thing to just snake his arms around her waist. She touched his arms with her fingers. Her chest was against his ribcage. She was skinny, thought Sandy. All skin and bone really. 'Promise that you won't let him turn you against me. Promise me, Sandy.' There were tears in her eyes. She put her head to his shoulder. He felt an erection swelling and pulled his hips back a little so that she would not feel it. He had been embarrassed more than once at school dances when a girl had noticed his erection during a slow dance and told her friends, who would then giggle at him for the rest of the night. He wanted there to be no mistakes with Rian.

'Don't get me wrong, Sandy,' she was saying. 'I don't want to give you the wrong impression. Robbie is my brother and I wouldn't hurt him for the world, but he's bitter at having had to look after me all this time. He feels he's losing out on life, and yet he won't leave me alone because he feels it's his job to look after me. There's a jumble of things in his head, but he *will* try to turn you against me. I know he will. He's tried it before.' Sandy wanted to ask her a question then, but she gave him no opportunity. 'He'll do anything. He'll tell any lies he wants to. Don't believe them.' As he held her waist, her hair tickled the backs of his wrists. Her hair was longer than he had imagined. It reached down to her waist and beyond. He looked down at her cowering head, resting so easily upon him.

'I promise,' he said, 'if you'll kiss me.' It was easily

said, as if he were dreaming. He felt like running away or making a joke of it, but something made him hold his ground. She looked at him and he could feel her eyes as they overwhelmed him. Everything he was, everything he had decided he would be in life, it all went out of the window in one easy fall. She kissed him. It was a slow, steady kiss, breathy. She seemed at ease, which unnerved Sandy slightly. He opened his eyes for a peek and saw that hers were open and rigidly upon him, studying him coldly. He closed his again quickly. It was as if his mother had found him to be feigning sleep. Her lips tasted of soap. He shrugged off the comparison and tried to enjoy himself. He should have been enjoying himself. It should have been heaven. Later it would seem as though it *had* been, but the moment itself was too curious and strained to be anything other than strange. He accepted its strangeness. He accepted everything. She breathed in his ear.

'Oh, Sandy,' she said. Then she pulled away from him, looking into his eyes as if uncertain of something. Eventually she forced herself to smile, and Sandy felt that she was depending on him for something profound, something beyond his immediate grasp. He felt a tiny weight of responsibility being shifted on to his shoulders. Did Robbie feel it too, inversely?

He watched her as she turned from him and began climbing the drainpipe. She was a small, brittle-boned monkey. He admired her long arms, the way her feet dug into what purchase the wall would afford. Her hair swung in rhythm with her body. Her skirt was flailing too, and suddenly, as he had not dared to hope, he was looking up inside it. She was calling something to him, but it was lost, like a distant voice calling across a swelling tide. Up inside it. The pants soiled but feminine. The tuft of hair crawling from beneath the cotton. A flush went through his whole body. He tried to control it. Useless; he had come. Oh God, he had never done that before, not standing up, not in his denims. His legs were as weak as if he had been swimming. He watched the boards appear in the window, covering that doorway. The house was closed again, dark, apparently lifeless. He trotted gingerly across the lawn and climbed his wall. The wet smell was all around him. He would have to take the quiet way home, and he hoped that he would meet no one. That kiss. Her saliva was still in his mouth. It was turning cold now. He had to get home, had to rush upstairs, ignoring his mother's call from the living room, and change into clean clothes. Perhaps he could have a bath. No, this was not his regular bath night. The water would not be warm, and his mother would suspect something. He would have to wash his trousers in the bath tomorrow morning while his mother cooked the breakfast. And his pants. Her pants. That kiss. It went home with him, becoming more than it had been at the time with every step as the imagination took over. For once he hoped that Mr Wallace would be there. That would keep his mother occupied while he ran upstairs. Rian. He would watch Robbie. He would listen closely to any accusation, and would challenge any lie. Rian was his girlfriend after all. He had to protect her. She was depending on him.

4

Dear Mary,

Sorry I've been so long in replying. The job is as hectic as ever. That's the only excuse I can offer, and I don't suppose it's a very good one at that, but I hope you will forgive me as ever! I'm glad to hear that you are winning the Adolescent War with young Sandy. Give him my best wishes, will you? He must be real man-sized by now. Could you maybe send me a photo of the two of you? I keep meaning to find a recent photograph of myself to send on, but you know what it's like. I think I've changed a bit since the last photo I sent you. That was Christmas 1980 if my memory serves me right. Or was it '79? The brain cells have given up the battle! Only the body soldiers bravely on. There are few new victories. I sit behind my desk all day signing my name to scraps of paper. Sometimes I am allowed out of my chair to walk around one of the sites. You would think I have an important job, huh? Sometimes I even fool myself that I do have an important job. Truth is, I'm no more than a glorified clerk. I wish I was out on the sites again, running things out there rather than in this little box. (Yes, I'm writing to you from my place of work. This is the company's stationery.) Old Emerson himself was in to see me last week. That's the first time I've seen him since they promoted me, which apparently means that I'm doing fine, or at least making no visible botches. Emerson nodded his head a few times and grunted and then asked if I was getting married yet. He's been asking me that for four goddamn years! One day I'll maybe surprise him, but I think not. I'm a born bachelor, I guess, so it's no use you hounding me to get hitched either!

This schoolteacher guy sounds okay. You have my blessing, sis, whatever you decide. I suppose you feel you have to think of Sandy just now, but he'll soon be flying the roost himself. You're only thirty-one, Mary. In your last letter you sounded like some fifty-year-old. Get out there and grab some guy! Enjoy yourself while you're young. Look at me, I'm all of thirty-three, still single, still having an okay time with my decreasing band of merry bachelor men. There are lots of nice men around, Mary, so there's no excuse for you. If I could I'd swim the Atlantic and marry you myself . . . but of course I don't have the time! (Just joking, sis!)

Have you asked Sandy about his coming over to Canada for a holiday this year? I still think it would be a good idea – and no, I'm not trying to steal him! But maybe he could strike it lucky here like his Uncle Tom did. (Okay, so I'm no Howard Hughes.) Anyway, it would do him good to have a break after his exams. He needs time to think over his future, don't you think? And it would also give The Teacher and you some well-earned time by yourselves. Please think it over. For this year only! Super special offer. Much reduced prices. Hell, we're giving the stuff away. Canada doesn't have

78

an incredible amount going for it as a holiday centre, but there are parts of it I'd still like to see myself, parts I'm sure Sandy would enjoy. Way up north. Remember I went lumberjacking up that way when I first arrived here? What an experience that was. I only lasted four days! And I promise to keep Sandy out of mischief if he comes. You have a bachelor's word on that! (Worth a grand total of not much.)

How's the money working out? Don't take any nonsense from that bloody bank manager, and please remember that you have my money in the account as a standby. I would be really grateful if you would feel that you can freely use it. I told you. It has been arranged with the bank for ages. I'll never touch that money, I don't need it, and I'm sure Mum and Dad would have wanted you to take it. I know they would. Please.

Well, Mary, I'm being allowed out of doors for a breath of fresh construction-site air in five minutes, so I better finish this. It was real nice to get your letter, Mary. Thanks. And keep them coming. Also, tell Sandy that if he doesn't write to me soon I will do something drastic to him while he sleeps! And all my love to him as well as to your good, good self. Closing for now.

All my love, Tom.
xxx

5

The daytimes glazed through the rest of the spring, blowing warm winds and the smell of grass into the nostrils of those still aware enough to appreciate such things. Everything opened up into the transient summer. Sandy would rise early, afraid of oversleeping for his exams. He took them seriously, and did an hour's revision before breakfast. Then, leaving his mother at the door, he would choose a stone to kick all the way to school.

The examination hall was stuffy and full of smiling, unserious contenders. He feared to look up in case his attention should be distracted and his crammed memory evaporate entirely. He had been storing rote answers for weeks. It needed only one of Belly Martin's funny faces to knock a dozen equations from his head. So he kept his eyes on the desk, though the air near the wood was dank and overpowering. Here was his school career: scrawls on a scratched desktop; a rickety chair; a list of multiple-choice questions; a one-in-five chance; feet sliding over the dusty tiled floor. One teacher sat at the front of the hall reading his newspaper. Another stared out of a window as he paced the rows of desks. This was it. Everything. It was ludicrous.

Nothing about it equated with ten years of schooling. Sandy was suddenly glad that he had swotted – not that he meant to stay on, but grades mattered. It had been drummed into him until it had seemed as casual a knowledge as the gospel stories he had known as a child, and like them this new knowledge – not knowledge, but *facts* pure and simple – would be forgotten in time.

The examinations weren't too difficult. Between them there were days of nothing, a time to laze and to taste freedom and to study the few sentences which constituted a distillation of several years' teaching. Sandy carried his lists of important sentences and equations around with him. He would take a list from his pocket and study it at random moments. These nuggets replaced, for a few weeks, his collection of good stones.

After each exam he was pleasantly surprised to feel himself drained and in need of sleep. He would go home and doze in the chair until tea-time. On waking, he would be unable to recall many of the exam questions. He would delete from his lists the information no longer needed, then would take the examination paper from his pocket and examine it as if it were an alien object. He could not have answered it. It would not seem the same paper that he had so recently sat. Even the words would be unfamiliar. It was a curious sensation, and one which others experienced. Belly Martin laughed at them when they discussed it one day.

'You're fucked then, aren't you? When that happens it means you haven't been concentrating.

You might have written anything down. Serves you right, you fucking swots. What good will it do you when we leave? There's no jobs anyway. Why bother?'

Belly Martin's stomach sagged obscenely over his waistband, and his pudgy fingers would lift leftovers from a neighbour's school-dinner plate straight into his gaping mouth. Fat boys are usually ridiculed at school, both in comics and in reality, but Belly was too ghastly to have even that fate befall him. He was not the archetypal fat boy. Indeed, Sandy often shuddered when he contemplated the differences. Belly was vicious. He would hug you to him in a clinch and would crush your face against his chest, smothering you. His shirt smelled of vinegar, as if he had not washed for a long time. He lied and stole and cheated, and if confronted by a teacher would retreat into the guise of typical fat boy – picked on, unloved, unwanted, innocent. To the frustration of his classmates, it was a part he played to perfection. He would spread his arms wide plaintively, and his eyes and mouth would open in astonishment, then he would blurt out his controlled acting until the teacher frowned and looked again for a culprit. Belly would soon be grinning, and would reach a hand deep into his trouser pocket, wriggling it around until he found some ancient paper-covered sweet. This he would crunch into tiny pieces, still laughing and slavering mild taunts at those who had informed on him.

'Ha! Better luck next time, clipes. Go tell fucking teacher. Ha!'

Sandy was revolted by the boy and always had been. He seemed impervious to pain, either mental or physical, like a lumbering dinosaur. That was the frustrating thing. Sandy tried not to be sitting near him in the examination hall. Belly scratched his bemused face with a rasping sound like the unwrapping of a difficult toffee and made life unbearable for those around him.

Revenges, often colossal in intent, were planned against him, but were never carried through with any degree of success. Sandy had planned several of his own. The simplest was the braining of Belly with an empty bottle in a dark alley. The most complex involved pieces of machinery, a trifle containing ground glass, and a nest of rats. Sandy used to keep these plans in a stolen jotter in his secret drawer at home, but he had guiltily torn them up just before his exams in case there was a God and it or he or she decided to spite him with low marks. It had been childish anyway. Any worthwhile revenge would be simple and short-winded. But what? That was the problem.

After the final examination, Economics, a few of them went down to the park with a carry-out filched from Colin's father's drinks cabinet. They leapt what had once been the hot burn – now a sorry old thing, dehydrated, its clay a raw, rusty colour – and jogged across the playing field in the direction of a small pond in the Wilderness. They carried the cans of warm lager inside their rolled-up jackets. They were so nearly men, only weeks away from the dole and the free money that came with it.

All except Sandy.

'Christmas!' yelled Colin. 'Christ's Mass! Sandy's got to stay on till Christmas!' As Sandy wiped his damp forehead he found it impossibly difficult to envisage snow and being wrapped up in layers of clothes and rushing to the fireside. It seemed too ludicrous an idea to have any grounding in the real world. He became disorientated, and almost asked his companions if they really believed in something as alien as snow. Then his head cleared a little, just in time for him to realise that they were crossing the pipeline over the river. He watched the others playing at being acrobats as they walked over the slender cylinder, then walked across himself, his legs trembling. They were waiting on the other side, laughing and pleading with him to fall off. He tried to smile, but kept looking down at the long green tendrils of weed in the water below. Once over, he leapt from the pipe on to crumbly brown earth. It was a good feeling. They jogged the rest of the way through the field to a pool of algae-covered water. Immediately one of them, Clark, stripped, and penis waving like a comedian's wand ran into the pond. He shrieked, but no one told him to be quiet. They were truly in the wilds here. No one would hear them shout or laugh or scream. Clark splashed out of the pool, green tapioca clinging to his white body. He scratched it away with a look of disgust.

'It's freezing in there,' he said. 'Dare you.' He looked around, but the rest of them were busy opening cans and catching the foam in their mouths.

He wiped himself with his T-shirt. 'Fair shares,' he said, walking towards them.

They lay in the long grass and stared at the sky as if it were a picture-show. They had blades of grass in their mouths. It was a time for lazing. They had spent their energy fighting in the pool.

'The dole in eight weeks,' said Clark. 'I can't believe it.'

'It would be better if we all had jobs, though,' said Colin.

'Ach, we'll get jobs eventually,' said Mark. 'We've deserved our rest. Complete rest and relaxation. No early rises except when you've to sign on. It's just what the doctor ordered.'

'Oh aye?' said Sandy. 'Seeing the doctor, are you, Mark? I wonder what for?'

'The clap if I know him.'

'Now, now, lads. Let's not be too hasty in condemning the poor sod. Let's condemn him *slowly*.'

'Ha fucking ha,' said Mark.

'Any advance on that?' said Sandy.

'But seriously, guys. No more school! It's like being let out of jail after doing thirty years' hard labour.'

'Now, now, Mark. Remember one of us has to go back.'

'Oh yes. Sorry, Witchy. I forgot.'

'I don't like being called Witchy, Marcus.'

'I don't like being called Marcus, Witchy.'

Sandy stuck a hand up into the air and Mark clasped it. They shook. Then there was silence for a time. Sandy lay with his shirt crumpled over his genitalia. They had to be protected, he had told his friends, as you never knew when they would come in handy. Sandy worked hard at every utterance he made in this group. His jokes were his defence in a way, and were also what had first gained him entrance to the gang. He did not want to lose his privilege.

'Freedom,' said Clark. 'It's okay, Sandy. You don't have any exams when you go back. No work to do. Just sit it out, like you were in jail in Monopoly.' Everyone chuckled, grass still wedged between teeth. The sun was too bright. It made Sandy's eyes dizzy to look at it. He watched the blood red of a foetus form whenever he closed his eyelids.

'That little shit Belly Martin. It's about time somebody got him. And good, too. Give him something as a souvenir.'

'You're right, Colin. But how?' They thought for a few moments.

'Bring him down here,' said Sandy, savouring the words as they formed inside his aching head, 'and throw him in the pond. Then leave him, naked, wet, lost in the dark, and just go home.' Somebody sat up. Their shadow blocked the sun. Sandy peered up but could not see who it was.

'That's brilliant, Sandy. But how do we capture him?' said Colin.

'Kidnap him some evening when he leaves the chip shop,' said Sandy, closing his eyes again.

'It's a fine plan,' Clark said lazily.

'A great plan,' said Colin. Everybody agreed. 'So

great that I think we should have a trial run!' Colin was on Sandy immediately. Sandy gasped, nearly choking on his blade of grass. He clung with one hand to his shirt while the other clawed at the earth. Colin was dragging him by the feet towards the pond. Too late, Sandy released his grip on the shirt and grabbed for Colin. With a splash, he had been thrown in a semi-circle right into the pond. He was going down. It seemed incredibly deep, and certainly much deeper than it had been twenty minutes before. It was like being tossed into the sea from a helicopter. Sandy turned and turned. He sucked in some liquid and began spluttering. The water was sour for a second and then was bland, filling his mouth, trickling down his resisting throat. It was dark down there, but he fought against the darkness. His feet touched bottom. He pushed hard, and his head rose above the surface. Someone was shouting.

'By Christ! Here comes the Loch Ness Monster!'

He stood coughing and retching for a minute. They were at the edge of the pool and began to help him out. They could see that something quite frightening had just happened.

'Sorry, Sandy,' said Colin, patting his back. 'It was just a joke. Are you all right?' Sandy nodded.

'Fine,' he said. Then, tipping his body slightly forward over the pool, he brought up a foamy concoction of lager and lemonade and algae and water. The others stood back a little.

'Well,' said Mark, 'we'll not be swimming in there for a while.'

They lay down again and were reflective for some

time. Sandy stared at the grass and let himself dry in the hot sun. He felt fine, but shaky.

'Are you still seeing Shona McKechnie?' Mark asked Colin. This brought an interested glint to every eye: sex.

'Well, lads,' said Colin, 'that's confidential. Hush-hush. I wouldn't like to say, really.'

'That means she's chucked him in,' said Clark, hoping it were true.

'Just you keep thinking that, young Clark, if you want to.'

'Well, tell us then, Colin.'

'Okay, boys. Are you sitting comfortably?' They shifted closer to Colin. 'Once upon a time,' he began, 'there was a sexy young lad called Colin McLintock. Now, Colin happened to stumble across a ravishing princess one day . . .'

'Stumbled is the right word! You were pissed as a fart.'

'Okay, Mark,' said Colin angrily, '*you* tell the story.' But they poked Mark in the ribs and pleaded with Colin to continue. 'No more interruptions then,' he said. 'Now, as I was saying, this handsome lad one day met a lady at a party, and the lady's name was Shona McKechnie. They enjoyed one another's company, and started necking on the couch. He walked her home. There was a passionate goodnight kiss on her doorstep, and that, thought Colin, was that. But no! It was not to be, my children. For, as it turned out, this Shona person had a fiery reputation with the older boys in town. After school, it turned out, she would go up into the

Wilderness and cavort with the whole of the Cars gang. Word had got around that Shona had the hots for noble young Colin, and so the Cars, in their infinite stupidity, decided to scare him away from the princess, a bit like the Ugly Sisters in "Cinderella" . . .'

'Christ, Colin, you better watch that they're not hiding in the grass this very minute. If they could hear you . . .'

'So,' Colin's voice became even louder, 'the aforementioned Cars gang, being a cowardly bunch of shits, chased poor Colin for weeks and would be waiting for him outside school, forcing him to sneak home by devious routes, and they made his life hell to the extent that he gave up seeing Shona, though she still chased him in school. So you see, lads, he was in a tight spot. Chased by *two* fearsome elements.' Colin was on his feet now, acting with gusto. 'What could he do? He did what a man must do.'

'Quite right,' said Sandy.

'He started seeing Shona again, but making certain that it was kept as secret as was humanly possible. He told only his most trusted friends. And, my most trusted friends, he is still seeing her. He is seeing her tonight, he thinks. And he is regularly getting his nuts from her.'

'You jammy bastard,' said Mark.

'What's she like then, Colin?' asked Clark.

'Princesses are not to be discussed in such terms,' said Colin, sitting down again. There were groans of dissent.

Sandy knew these games. They were old, and

their utility value, as the Economics exam would have had it, seemed to decrease with each rendition. They all knew what sex was. They had learned about it from boys with older brothers, from glossy magazines flicked through in public conveniences, from tentative dates at parties and school discos. But probably, despite all their bravado, Colin was the only one of them who had properly lost his virginity. The rest of them were left straining on the leash like bug-eyed dogs. Sex for them was the toilet at home or under the sheets with a handkerchief and the mild queasiness and guilt afterwards. The horror that your mother would find or had already found some telltale stain. Not all the boys at school were as innocent. The Cars, the town's gang, were not innocent, but then they were mostly older boys who had already left school.

Sandy picked a new blade of grass and chewed it, crushing the sap with his teeth. He thought of his own princess. Dark golden kisses, treasured like jewels. He had written some poetry for her, but would never let her see it. What if she couldn't read? All the better: the poem was terrible.

From the falling time you call to me,
From the youngest time you call to me,
And now we are here,
Shed not a tear,
From the falling time.

Your hair is so long
I feel I could climb it,

Into a castle where treasure is hidden.
Your shape is as secret as the key to that treasure.
Will you give me the key,
For this is a tempting time?

He was embarrassed by it, but he would keep it in his secret drawer beside the others and the stories he had written and hope his mother did not find it. His friends would laugh at him if they found out. All they knew was that he was good at writing stories and poems when asked to in English by a teacher who was going out with his mother.

He had visited the mansion one day in every week for a while now. He was waiting for Rian to suggest some meeting in a secret place. She had not yet done so. He had to content himself with a stolen kiss when Robbie was not around, and then only if Rian were in the mood. If not, she would sit with her face as dark as a coal-box and her arms folded firmly across her chest. On those days he would talk more with Robbie, and be more friendly towards him, just to spite his cruel princess.

They were talking about videos now – about the ones they had seen lately and the ones they would see when their parents were out. Sandy thought that he would leave and go to the Soda Fountain. Mr Patterson had promised him a whole lot of chocolates when he had finished his exams. But Sandy did not eat many sweets these days. Their taste was debilitating. It slowed him down, making his insides all sugary and numb. He preferred fruit. He would visit the fruit shop. But then he was being asked a question.

'What about you, Sandy? You never had a dad, did you? I mean, you never knew who your dad was?' They were talking about someone whose father had died suddenly. Now they had directed the conversation towards him. He looked at the serious faces and the acne and the thin, pallid bodies.

'No,' he said, 'I never knew.'

'Did you ever try to find out? Didn't you ever ask your mum?'

'No.'

How could he have done that? It had taken time to discover that children ought to have a father. By the time he found out, he had become sad for his mother. How could he have asked her such a personal and unnecessary question? Often, though, he had thought of asking her. He knew some of the rumours which had been currency when he was a child. It was his Uncle Tom, who had then quickly scarpered. It was the Devil himself, and his mother was a witch after all. It was one of his Uncle Tom's friends. It was a fairy king. Would she tell him if he asked? Perhaps she would, now that he had grown up, but what did it matter? It was a moment's curiosity every few months. It was nothing.

'What's it like then, not having a dad?'

'It's not like anything really. It's not very different.'

'How can you know if you've never had one in the first place?' Colin was good at arguing. Sandy was forced to shrug his shoulders.

'Well, it doesn't seem any different,' he said. 'Am I different from you?'

'Well, you're witchy for a start,' said Clark, laughing.

'I'd put a spell on you if I was,' said Sandy. 'I'd change you from a frog.' They all laughed at that. Sandy felt safe again. He was tempted to visit the mansion, but he knew that it would probably be empty at this time of the day. It was tempting, too, to visit the gypsy encampment at Craigie Hill. It would only take ten minutes from the Soda Fountain. The wind was beginning to blow a bit anyway. They could not lie here for much longer. Sandy pressed a finger down on to some of his goosebumps. They flattened for a second, then swelled. The dark strands of hair on his arms stood on end when he shivered, like the sea rolling up to the esplanade in Kirkcaldy.

'Why don't we go to Kirkcaldy?' he suggested.

'No money,' said Clark. Colin and Mark nodded.

'Well, let's arrange a trip for when we have money. To celebrate the end of the exams. We can go to the Harbour Tavern. Dicky Preston says they serve you in there even if you're underage. He says it's easy.'

'Okay,' said Colin. The others were nodding. 'That sounds fine. We'll need a good bit of cash, though, so start hunting through your mum's purse and looking in your dad's pockets. Okay?'

'Magic.'

6

The cemetery sat at the top of The Brae. It was quite large, sprawling with the headstones of mining accidents and many other less newsworthy deaths. Matty Duncan was buried here in an untended but often visited corner. Mary passed this corner, and glanced at the gravestone. *If he hadn't died, it would have been my father . . .*

The cemetery contained most of Mary's family. A lot of plots had gone untended for too long, and yellow-flowering weeds were beginning to make serious inroads, giving the place a rank, lush look and a constant pungency resembling that of urine.

Mary stooped over one or two graves on her way to her parents' plot, and pulled up some of the silent, stubborn weeds. Seldom did they come up at the roots. Mary knew that hers was merely temporary surgery.

Her parents' tombstone gleamed still. In a few years it would lose its shine, but not yet. The letters were dull gold and indented clearly. Mary squatted by the graveside and placed her posy of flowers on the grass. She lifted the two glass jars from either side of the tombstone. There were partly withered stalks in one. The other was empty, someone having taken the flowers she had placed in it so delicately last week. She said nothing and thought nothing, just walked with both jars over to a small hut beside which stood a bin and a cold-water standpipe. She emptied the stalks into the bin where they landed on top of other matted and decaying vegetation, and rinsed out both jars under the tap before filling them. The icy water lingered on her hands, freezing them, sending all feeling to some foreign region. She blew on her fingers, trying to warm them, as she carried the jars over to the graveside, her parents, and the small tribute of flowers.

Having placed the jars in their original positions, marked by the greener grass beneath each, Mary made herself comfortable on the slightly damp ground at the foot of the grave and smiled. She had not smiled for a long time. She seemed to be studying the plot, just as she would have studied a work of careful embroidery. When she was satisfied with the arrangement of the graveside, she began to speak in a soft, respectful voice.

Clouds moved overhead with a regal gait befitting the calm afternoon. Crows were arguing in the distance, probably in the trees of the kirkyard. She told this to her mother. Her mother was interested in details and in the kind of day it happened to be, in the sights and sounds from which she had been banished. Mary's mother had been a nature-lover all her years, taking the children out for long rambles on Sunday afternoons, summer evenings, and school holidays. She would point out wild flowers and trees to her two children, telling them the names of each and making them repeat these names so that they would remember. Then, later in the walk she would suddenly ask, 'What was that called again?', pointing to something, and when they shouted out the answer she would chuckle and say that they seemed to have learned more that day than in a whole week's schooling.

They would laugh together and rush down the steep hill hand in hand and shrieking, collapsing eventually into the sofa at home, the sweat on their brows linking them inexorably to the day's events, making them grin and glance at the father who pretended not to mind being excluded from their group.

Those were days of near innocence, days which all too soon had become irretrievably the past. She never talked with her dead mother about the day when she had been thrown into the hot burn, or about the days that followed. Those times sat in crouched silence in Mary's mind, grinning rictus-like and festering.

She spoke with her mother of flowers and brooks and country walks, of a land which might once have existed but was now no more. Her father listened in silence, doubtless impressed by their relationship, sisters more than mother and daughter, sharing their thoughts and their vision like girls tucked beneath the bedclothes in a darkened room. Her father would nod and listen, but make no comment other than to grunt when spoken to. He seemed further away than her mother, and Mary knew the reason why. His face had vanished from her memory, leaving only the vague outline of a shuffling, heavy man with a pipe clamped between his teeth. But Mary knew her mother's face better than she knew her own. It was kindness and russet cheeks and a cold compress on a headache. It was love. It was love that she talked to now as she sat by the cool graveside and stroked the bristles of grass as if they were long weavings of hair.

Blushing like a schoolgirl, she told her mother about Andy.

'Yes, Mum, he's lovely. He really cares for me. He's always doing little things like bringing me chocolates or flowers. Like an old-fashioned suitor in a way. He has a car and we go out into the country sometimes to little pubs and interesting places. People look at us as if we were man and wife.' She paused. 'I think maybe one day we will be. Sandy's still growing, though he says he isn't. He's sitting his exams at school just now. He's been swotting for weeks. He comes home exhausted. Mind you, he's still quite a laddie. He's out till all hours some nights. No, I'm being strict enough with him, Mum, but you have to give them a bit of freedom these days or they go off the rails. He never gets into trouble. I think he's got himself a girlfriend. He blushes like a schoolgirl when I ask him.' She chuckled. 'I don't know who it is yet. I just hope it's someone nice and not one of those tarty young things that hang around down the street. But I think Sandy's got enough sense not to get into trouble in that respect.'

She was silent for a few moments. The crows continued their dialogue. Smaller birds began bickering in some bushes nearby. 'The birds are fairly singing today, Mum. I can't really tell what kinds of bird. There are crows and sparrows, of course, but goodness knows what else. You would know them all. I've forgotten all those bird-songs that you taught Tom and me. Tom's fine, by the way. I had a letter from him recently. Have I seen you since? I forget. My memory seems to be going a bit haywire these days. Sandy's leaving school. He's adamant about that. I wonder what he'll do with himself. If you were here, Mum, he'd listen to your advice. He takes little or no notice of his own mum. Independent as anything, and still only fifteen. Fifteen, Mum.' She paused as if listening to something. 'Yes, Mum, it has been the ruin of me. But I love my Sandy and I wouldn't not have had him. I can't think of such a thing. What do you think, Dad? What do you think?' She was weeping now. She rose to her feet and, drying her eyes on a delicate handkerchief, walked quickly from the grave. The flowers in their jars trembled in the slight breeze.

As Mary left the cemetery, she saw George Patterson toiling up The Brae. She took to her heels and ran, dodging into the housing scheme so as not to be seen by him.

Mr Patterson was going home for lunch. He had shut the Soda Fountain at half past one, aware that young Sandy was not going to show up after his exam. It was a beautiful afternoon and quiet. He was glad of the fresh air. The shop was a tomb as far as he was concerned. He was selling less than ever, which meant smaller profits, but more importantly fewer customers with whom to while away the time. George Patterson was in his fifties and was waiting to die. It was a slow process. He ate packets of sweets and smoked cigarettes and drank himself silly in isolation, but still he could not die. Perhaps this hill would do the trick.

George Patterson wanted to die because he could not see that it could be worse than living. He went to church sometimes, but no longer believed in God. It made it easier for him to want to die. All he wanted was not to exist. That he was liked in the town only made it harder. He wanted to be hated, but people would not let him be hated. What was worse, he would not let himself be hated. When he met people, he would feel a smile appearing on his face, though he willed himself to frown, to hurl abuse. He found himself forced to make noble gestures, all the time hating himself, all the time aware of the grossest hypocrisy.

Mr Patterson was a bachelor. He lived alone in a small house in Cardell, on the outskirts of town. He read lots of magazines and newspapers there and listened to the radio. He had no pets. He had no housekeeper. He tidied the house himself and did his own washing and ironing. He was portly from having eaten too many sweets during his lifetime, but was not entirely unfit. That he was also bald and ruddy-faced merely added to the endearment others felt towards him. He hated it all. This world was a mockery, and human beings were mockeries of life. Another flood was needed, if there had been a first, a flood to wash away all the debris, to leave only a handful of starry-eyed children and the few good people who had to exist somewhere. George Patterson would have prayed for that, had he still believed in God. Being an unbeliever, he merely thought about it.

He sweated his way towards his shaded house and hoped that the pain in his side would not intensify. He passed the old minister, or rather he made to pass him. The minister, as always, stopped to speak with one of his respected and respectable parishioners. One, admittedly, who was not seen at church as regularly as might have been expected, but who nevertheless showed the true Christian spirit.

'A lovely afternoon, Mr Patterson. Is this you just getting home for lunch?'

'Yes, Mr Davidson, I'm afraid so.' Mr Patterson loathed himself for his newly arranged smile and simpering tone. He came to a halt beside the old man with the cherub's face and the silver hairs curling from his nostrils telling everyone that he was a man of God but a hard man too, a man one could deal with realistically.

'And how is the sugar trade, Mr Patterson? Are you still corrupting our youth with your tooth-rot?' There was a smile on the old man's face, but his gaze was honest enough. Mr Patterson laughed uneasily.

'Everyone has their little sin, Mr Davidson. I'm not saying that sweets aren't bad for you, but there are other pleasures a lot worse.' The minister laughed heartily.

'True, very true, but it's a weak defence if defence it is. I would agree that there are degrees of temptation. I am often tempted by a dram now and then, but would certainly consider the yielding to such as something less heinous than being tempted to commit a crime and carrying through the act. But look at it another way. You are selling something you know to be bad . . .'

And so are you, old man, thought Mr Patterson in an evil moment, so are you.

'. . . so does that make you the better man?' Mr Patterson, lost in his thoughts, had missed some part of the minister's argument vital to its understanding. He smiled and shook his head.

'You've got me beat there, Mr Davidson. What do you want me to do? Sell my livelihood?' The minister laughed and shook his head. He took George Patterson's hand and patted it lightly. His clasp was soft and dry.

'Indeed no, George, I was only joking with you. You better away and get your lunch now. Don't be disheartened by the jabberings of an old man. Will we see you in church again soon?' The minister's eyes suddenly stopped their survey of the houses around them and concentrated themselves on those of Mr Patterson, who felt the blood tingling responsively in his cheeks.

'Yes indeed,' he said as keenly as he could, 'probably this weekend in fact. I've been rather busy, you see . . .' This time the minister patted his shoulder.

'No need for excuses, George. Only too glad to have you come when you can manage. I look forward to seeing you. Maybe I'll drop in for some of your pandrops sometime.'

'Please do,' said Mr Patterson, walking away. Old bugger, he thought to himself. He'll want them on the house if he does. Still, the old minister wasn't a bad sort. Quite wicked in his own way, always berating people for their occupations or preoccupations or sins of indulgence. He was in a right nest of vipers here. Carsden stank of corruption. Mr Patterson remembered it as it had been, or at least had seemed, when he had been young. Times had been hard, yes, but the people had been honest and generous. People, after all, were all that towns had going for them. Mr Patterson had fallen as far as anyone, and further than many. No one knew the sins he had committed. People thought him the salt of the earth. He smiled bitterly as he walked the rest of the way home. If only he could die. He could not commit suicide: he was too much of a coward for that. He wanted – needed – to die naturally, but quickly. Let him die quickly.

The very next morning, Mr Patterson learned from his first customer that the old minister had died in his sleep. He shook his head in disbelief. So this was the world. The bitter irony overtook any idea of immediate mourning. It was as if a malevolent creator had decided to show him something of its truly impersonal power. He stood behind the old wooden counter all day and heard nothing but good spoken of the man. He dipped his hand into many glass jars of coloured sweets and guiltily filled many

102

paper bags. No one bought pandrops. Pandrops were for the kirk on a Sunday.

Sandy came in at four o'clock for a haircut. Mr Patterson was silent much of the time, forgetting about the sweets he had promised the boy. He made a good job of his fringe, however. Afterwards, Sandy asked for a quarter of pandrops for his mother. Mr Patterson stared hard at him. It was like staring at his own conscience magnified many times. He should have said something more to the old man. Too late now, too late. He should have said much, much more to the old minister. He gave Sandy the mints and would not take the proffered money.

7

TUES

For over a week he had not seen her. It was like something gnawing inside his stomach. He thought that he might have an ulcer or something, but did nothing about it, afraid that it would be true. He sat in his bedroom much of the time and scribbled on pieces of paper and in old jotters. He read a lot of books from the library. When his mother told him off mildly for sitting indoors when it was so warm outside, he would silently pick up his books and switch off his record-player and trot downstairs. He would sit sullenly on the doorstep with a book held close to his face while his mother watched his protest in mounting frustration. He was becoming a zombie to her. She was worried, naturally, but could think of no way to ask him what the trouble was without him clamming up even more than he already had. She again wished that her mother was alive. She wished that she herself had been a stronger mother when Sandy was growing up. She wished a lot of things. Then she would get on with her housework.

Sandy sat on the step. He boiled like an egg in a simmering pan. It was an unpleasant heat. It made him tired and unable to think. He had to squint at his book because of the sun, and that gave him a headache. He could not win. He was reading a quite funny American novel. He guffawed at a few of the jokes. That was as far as a laugh could force itself from his body. He thought about Rian. He fantasised about her, and always in his fantasies she was not the Rian he knew but some wilder, more animal figure. She bit and scratched and connived. Robbie looked over her shoulder into Sandy's face as Sandy pulled her to the ground and she laughed. These images scared him, and made him uneasy about the true relationship between sister and brother (he remembered the rumours about his own mother and *her* brother), but at the same time he was gloriously in love with the new version of Rian, a girl who would know things he needed to know and who would teach him the rules of new games. She pulled on his hair as she twisted his face towards hers. He champed like a tethered horse to go to the mansion. His exams had kept him away at first, and then he had been made to visit an ill and very old grand-aunt in Leven. He might have gone today, but something held him back – the self-imposed tether. Tomorrow he was going to Kirkcaldy on the expedition planned a few days ago. He had taken some money out of his small bank account for that.

His mother brought him a glass of lemonade, though he had not asked for it. She placed it on the doorstep, while his body tensed.

'There you are,' she said. He stared at his book. He thought for a second of ignoring the glass, of not drinking it. She was always doing things like that for him. Then he gave in.

'Thanks, Mum,' he said, listening to the ice-cubes tinkling as he lifted the glass. His mother was smiling as she stepped back into the kitchen. She thought that perhaps a small victory had been won.

Sandy sipped the sweet drink and felt his teeth going grainy immediately. Plaque, that was the enemy. He did not want false teeth. He tried drinking without letting the liquid linger in his mouth, and coughed when some fizz went up his nose. He examined his breath by breathing out through his mouth and then in through his nose very quickly. His breath did not smell too bad. He had some spots, though. He would have to start shaving soon, and then his spots would get worse. Thankfully, he did not have any trouble with his hair. It was dry and thick. It never ran to grease like Colin's or Belly Martin's, which was a miracle considering the amount of chips he ate. He had read in a girls' magazine at school about the causes of acne: fatty substances, sweets, not washing properly. The same things did for the hair too, apparently. He washed often, yet whenever he scratched with his fingernails across his face he would find grey grime beneath the nails. This he would scrape out with the edge of a tooth and spit on to the ground. He would look in the mirror. He would look sparkling clean. He would scrape his nose with a fingernail. There would be dirt beneath the nail again. It astonished him. How did Rian wash? Did she ever? She did not smell, except for the sweetish smell of grass, so he

106

supposed that she did. Perhaps down at the edge of the river, or from the stand-pipe at the golf course. Yes, that seemed obvious. Then it struck him: she must wash either early in the morning or else late at night so as not to be seen. Someone hiding in the gorse could watch her, could meet her.

Could watch her washing.

Another fantasy revolved in the hot sun, and in it Rian was the Rian he hoped for, and Robbie was nowhere to be seen. He left his book and his lemonade and returned to his room.

Mary lifted a stool out of the kitchen and on to the doorstep. She flopped down on it and raised her head towards the sun. She closed her eyes and felt the rays on her skin, burning and tingling and soothing. She opened her eyes and looked at the garden. It was in need of some work. She would ask Sandy, but not now, would tempt him with a pound. She used to give him threepence to go to the corner shop. That was a while ago now. Her mother had tempted him with biscuits and bread and butter and gooey strawberry jam. Times changed. It was a phrase overused but true. Times changed and people changed with them. She could have done with a man around the place when Sandy was younger, someone who would have taken him fishing or for long walks. Too late for that now. Now she needed a man for herself, alone as she would be in a year or two. It frightened her, but if Andy stayed it would be fine. It would be heaven. Tom was right: she needed a good man and she wasn't so old. The older you got the more you needed them in some respects. She smiled but the smile quickly disappeared, like a young animal in strange territory. Poor old Mr Davidson had died, and him such a fit-looking man usually. He had been good to her, had listened to her in the very worst times. He had given her the Church as a solid rock of fresh life, and she had clung to it ever since with the frantic scratching fingers of one who is near to losing her balance and falling off. To hell with the sneering congregation. She spoke to her God.

The Church mixed uneasily with some of the ideas handed down to her by her mother and her mother's mother, but she held both sets of beliefs dearly and would part with neither. Sandy had no religious sense at all. It saddened her. He had reneged on going to church when he was twelve and had not gone since except to weddings and funerals. When Mary looked around her on a Sunday she could see why. The pews were quarter full, and then with predominantly elderly people: the women in their ageing Sunday coats and 1950s hats; the men mouthing the hymns while their wives sang shakily. It was a drab spectacle. There were only a few young people dotted around. The young men sang lustily. Their cheeks were ruddy with righteousness. Some of them would glance at her bitterly. Now Mr Davidson was dead. Who would replace him? Someone younger, certainly, and someone who, being young, would please the older churchgoers less. If the congregation grew any smaller it would be embarrassing.

It was a good day for a walk, but Mary knew that Sandy would not go with her, and a walk by herself was a lonely thing. Andy had promised to drop by in the afternoon, school drawing to a close for the summer, and take her out. Perhaps he could be persuaded to go walking. They would have to drive some distance from the town before it would be possible for them to walk together without embarrassment, without the whispers and stares from the women in their long old-fashioned coats, bags hanging heavily from their arms. They would have to drive into the country, way out by Kinross. A car made all things possible, even escape. She would take a bath after lunch in case she had been sweating. The lavatory flushed upstairs. The pipes gurgled and the liquid ran into the underground system of sewers. There were countries worse than Scotland. If only lives could be made better through decent plumbing and housing. But life wasn't quite that simple, nor was it as concrete. Dig beneath the surface and you would not find a system of pipes and taps to be switched on and off; you would find, rather, wild depths, guilty feelings, an ever-changing geography. Mary shivered a little as a wind blew across her from the garden. Goosebumps appeared on her bare arms. She heard Sandy padding about upstairs and decided to go in herself.

'What do you fancy for lunch, Sandy? There's some cold meat and salad. Is that okay?' This she shouted from the bottom of the stairwell. She heard his reply from the distance of his room.

'Fine, Mum. Whatever you like.' She knew from

the tone that he felt she was intruding again, calling on him merely as a pretext to find out what he was up to. She did not care what he was up to.

'I'll leave everything on the table then, and you can help yourself when you feel hungry.' She waited. 'Okay?'

'Fine, Mum.'

If only she could understand him. If only he would open himself to her. Tom said in his letters that it was an adolescent thing. Everybody went through it. But who was Tom to know about that? He had never had to bring up a child.

'Have you written that letter to Uncle Tom yet, Sandy?'

'Not yet,' he answered impatiently. 'I'll do it this afternoon.'

Sandy had decided that he did not want to go to Canada, not this year. His mother had been mildly surprised by his rapid, unshakeable decision. 'Maybe next year,' he had said at the dinner table that evening. She had not pressed him for a reason, but he had given her one anyway. 'My pals,' he had said, 'this is maybe my last chance to see them before they all go off to get jobs and get married. They're all talking about moving away, so I'd like to spend the summer just seeing them.' His mother had nodded in silence and sipped her tea. Rian, he had been thinking, I'm not giving up Rian. Not when I can feel that she's so close. Maybe one day he could take *her* to Canada. Besides, it was true that he wanted to see Mark, Clark and Colin as much as possible. They had been good friends, and they would soon be leaving. The summer holiday promised lots of adventures together. Kirkcaldy. Edinburgh. Football. Fishing. Rian. It would be a great summer.

Sandy sat in his bedroom and thought about the minister dying and whether there was a God or not. He thought that it must be good to die believing that there was something after death. To have no belief was as scary a thing as he could think of. He considered the possibility of an afterlife. The idea of Heaven, of pearly gates and angels with harps, was unthinkable. But then what if that idea were merely a simplification, an analogy, because the idea of an afterlife proper was too difficult to explain? That might make sense. Sandy did not want to die, but death was around him at every moment. A vague friend had died in a car crash ten months before. Sometimes his sides ached for no reason and he lay in bed thinking that he was about to die. He did not want to go to church and pray and sing hymns, but it would be good to believe in life after death, life of any kind. The old minister had seemed a happy man. He had spoken with Sandy whenever he had met him. He had shaken his hand in a firm, dry grip, had patted his shoulder like Mr Patterson and had offered words of advice on things Sandy at the time had thought the man could know nothing of, like growing up, and being a scapegoat, and the like. Yet his smile had always been sincere and only a little patronising. What if he had known things Sandy had not? What if he *knew* rather than simply believed?

How could Sandy find out? There was no way. The old minister was dead. Then he had an idea. He knelt beside his bed, having first wedged a chair against the bedroom door, and began to whisper.

'Oh Lord, if there is an afterlife, if there is something after we die, then let the minister, Mr Davidson, talk to me. Let him come to me when I'm dreaming, or better still while I'm wide awake, and let him show me that there's an afterlife. If you do this, God, then I will believe in you and will go to church with my mother and suchlike. Amen.' He opened his eyes. He was a sinner, so maybe nothing would happen. But then, he thought, all the more reason for God to want to save him.

He would not visit Rian that evening and so would show his sincerity to any God that might be around. He reached under his bed, beneath the carpet, and pulled out one of his small collection of sex magazines. Deliberately, he tore it in half, then in half again. He rose from his floor and gazed out of the window. He saw a car pass. He saw a lamp-post. He saw the wasteland that stretched to the site of the old mine. He saw nothing that resembled God, and nothing that looked as if any hand of God had ever passed over it. He frowned. Was it all a trick? Should he go to the mansion anyway? No, he would stay put. He wondered if his mother would like to go for a walk up Craigie Hill. He left his room and started downstairs.

8

The alarm woke Sandy at seven thirty the next morning. He thrust a hand from beneath the bed-clothes and brought the clock into bed with him, fumbling to switch the bloody thing off. He stuffed it under his pillow and let it run down to a mechanical nothingness, then he drifted back into his dream. It was not a dream about Mr Davidson. It was a dream about Rian, a lengthy narrative dream. He was nearly sound asleep when he realised that this was the day they were all going to Kirkcaldy. He threw back the covers and, peeling open his eyes, swivelled out of bed.

Andy Wallace washed his car. His neighbours were just beginning to leave their homes for Saturday shopping trips. The sun was cool, but the sky promised a good day. Andy soaped the car's roof. Blimps of paint showed here and there where the rust was aching to break through. The car was a wreck, but it was all he could afford. If he coaxed it, and spoke nicely to it, it usually choked itself into some kind of life. His next-door neighbour smiled as she passed, an empty canvas shopping-bag tied to each of her hands. Her small son walked disconsolately a few feet behind her.

'But me want sweeties,' he moaned.

'I know what you'll get,' his mother warned.

Andy studied her back. She was young, still in her twenties, and her body was in good health. But, like all women in Carsden it seemed, her voice was coarse and she had no dress sense. Her jeans were tight, but not tight enough in the right places, and her high-heeled shoes made her wobble along the pavement. Her son appeared to be wearing grubby cast-offs. His shoes scraped the ground like flints. Andy watched the boy watching him, and turned his attention back to the car. Her husband was a television engineer. He was a gruff young man whose voice was often raised when at home. Andy hated using his own living room because of the noise from his neighbours'. Their television set was kept loud, lifting any conversation with it. The transistor radio, the vacuum-cleaner, the wails of the child. Andy preferred to use the small spare bedroom which he had turned into a sort of comfortable working office. A lot of his books were kept there, as were desk, chair, typewriter, and two extra speakers connected to the stereo in the living room. He was planning to decorate the house during the long holiday. Not that it looked bad as it stood, but there was something queasy about living with someone else's colour scheme.

The house itself had been a snip at twelve thou, the building society pleased to lend him the necessary money, but it had been a mistake. He should have moved somewhere with a bit of privacy, somewhere out in the country. Still, you took jobs where you could find them, and ditto houses. This was the first house that he had actually owned. During his time at university he had stayed in rented flats and bedsits, and in his last school he had lived in a horrendous bed-and-breakfast establishment with no freedom whatsoever, his landlady being one of those Sunday spinsters who would be found loitering outside his room and would go into the bathroom after him to check for any misdemeanour. Andy had often considered leaving something nasty for her to find, but she had been a good soul in some respects, always giving him a special breakfast, and did not warrant such mischief. At a party once, when he had been an undergraduate, some student vets from Edinburgh had arrived with a sack. Later, a female scream from the bathroom had rung out. The stiffened corpse of an Alsatian dog was found sitting in the bath, a cigarette dangling from its mouth, reeking of formaldehyde. It had been a good joke for those drunk enough to appreciate it at the time, but then it had not been Andy's bathroom.

Those had been good days, dead dogs aside. Only thirty now, he was feeling that it was downhill all the way nevertheless. Mary brightened his life to an extent, but sometimes, when soulful, he would think that he was getting old and had nothing before him but the schoolteacher's life of Sisyphus. He watched the process unfold before him. When given a class of thirteen-year-olds, fresh enough from primary school, there was still a spark there, both of creative drive and of trust. As the years grew with them, however, the mistrust formed, the interest died, and the values – debilitating homely values – of the parents and elders took over, dragging them down into safe mediocrity. He saw some of them occasionally after they had finished with their schooling. Other teachers, friends, said that it was the mark of a good teacher that his or her kids kept coming back for a chat. If that were true, then he was a good teacher. He could certainly feel the distaste of some of the school's older, disciplinarian teachers towards him.

'It doesn't pay, Mr Wallace, to become *too* familiar with the children, or at least to be *seen* to be familiar with them. It causes unrest, a breaking down of the authority by which we keep them in check.' That from the assistant headmaster, a stocky, balding man who had won some kind of medal in the Second World War and wore it to church on Sundays and who terrorised the children by showing them what he could do with his tawse to a stick of chalk. It was pathetic. It was worse than that. Authority could have no hold over ninety per cent of the kids. With the belt now banned, the disciplinarians saw chaos descending and had nothing to fall back on, too late to make friends with their pupils. The pupils these days were definitely out to break weak teachers. It was a war, but one which could be won, to a large extent, through arbitration. There had to be talking. He was not like George McNair, the History master, who challenged unruly pupils to fights after school on the playing field behind the main building. That was one way to earn respect, but what price failure? One day McNair would be beaten in one of his bouts. Where would he stand then? He had put himself up against a wall in an alley of his own making.

Andy bent down to wash the hubcaps and felt his stomach straining over his waistband. He did little exercise, though he helped out during football practice sometimes. This afternoon Mary and he might go for a drive, then a walk, depending on the weather. God, he wanted her. He wanted her badly. There had not been a woman in his life for many months. He needed more from Mary than her company and conversation. He needed to have her silver-black hair loose and hanging across his bared chest. He knew that there were real complications. It was one thing to see a pupil's mother, though even that was fraught, but to be her lover . . . Ah, if only Sandy were leaving school at summer. If only there wasn't the wait till Christmas. Still, now that the boy had finished with exams there could be no more accusations of grade-rigging. At least no one could threaten Andy's relationship with Mary via that device. All the same, it was a problem until Christmas.

The sun pressed its weight upon him. He squinted up into the sky. It was as blue as a sky could be, bluer than the sea outside Kirkcaldy. He smiled into it and hoped that it was a good omen. He straightened up and cracked his spine. He was way out of condition. He studied the house, his house. There were no chimneys on the houses in this estate. They looked like rows of Lego buildings. He was cleaning

117

his car in Legoland on a sunny Saturday morning. He shook his head and chuckled. He was not going to let anything get him down today. Not anything.

WED

When the bus pulled away, its new cargo rattled their way up the winding stairwell and sauntered to the very back of the upper deck. They slumped into their seats and turned their heads to watch Main Street disappear behind them. Old people, staggering under the weight of bags, looked distantly at the roaring vehicle. Children stared up at the upper deck. The boys made gestures from the window. They were going to Kirkcaldy for the day. They were the most important people in the world.

Sandy, though he would not let it be known, was not keen on going upstairs. For one thing, all the smokers were there, and the smell of cigarettes made him queasy. For another thing, he could not be sure what gangs would board the bus between Carsden and Kirkcaldy to challenge his right to be sitting at the very back of the bus. He kept one hand in the pocket which contained his money. He examined the dying and unhealthy faces around him, faces which stared from the grimy windows as if fixed to a television screen. These people were lost, as hollow as the most brittle sea-shells. Sandy thought of days when he had been taken to Kirkcaldy beach by his grandmother. They might go there today, but it would be in a different guise. Today he was part of a group, a gang. He would walk differently and talk differently and act altogether differently. Walking to the bus stop, they had fed from each other as if studying older men. They aped those they wished to be. They strained towards manhood like little waggy-tailed dogs towards bigger bitches in heat. Sandy smiled wickedly.

He wanted to escape all of this, yet he did not even know what 'this' was.

Mark had brought along ten cigarettes. He offered them round as if they were cigars at his daughter's wedding. Sandy couldn't not take one. He lit it, but sucked on the cylinder only feebly, exhaling without really having inhaled in the first place. Still his mouth tasted horrible. His stomach began to do its little travelling dance. It was always worst on buses. When he was a child his grandmother used to stand with him at the door of any bus he travelled on, telling him that he would not be sick, and he never was.

He examined the faces along the edge of the bus, studying their reflections in the glass. The sun streamed in, and the tiny openings of the windows caused the passengers to broil. One old man looked on to the countryside as if surprised by it. His head shook like a clockwork toy. Sandy thought to himself that this man must have seen a lot of things – the war, the hunger of the Twenties and Thirties, death, decay, a quickly changing world. What good had it done him? He looked as if he might die at any moment, not having comprehended half of what he had seen in his life. Waste. That was the keyword. Perhaps Sandy would write a story about it all when he returned home. It seemed an important enough

119

thing to write about. He wrote a lot of stories and poems in his room.

He tossed the stub of cigarette on to the dirty floor and crushed it underfoot. The others puffed slowly, drawing in the smoke as if it were life, holding it until their lungs demanded new oxygen, exhaling slowly, their eyes intent on the stream of blue. They were dragons. That was why they smoked. Sandy smiled again. Colin's mouth had broken out. Severe red patches of acne curved around his lips and chin. A few of the lumps had yellow heads. It was disgusting. Sandy had had the occasional spot, but the lotions his mother now bought for him ensured that he was not, as she had put it, scarred for life. He fingered his face now. He wet the tip of one fingernail and scratched around his nose. He examined the fingernail. A tiny rind of grey was trapped beneath it. He scooped it out with another nail and flicked it on to the floor. Clark and Mark, who sat between Colin and Sandy, discussed records they might buy. There seemed so many. Mark kept the cigarette packet on his lap, as if showing it off to anyone who cared to look. He shook the matchbox against his ear and hummed a pop song to its rhythm. Sandy looked at him and saw that Colin was looking too. They smiled at each other, and Colin put his finger to his skull. Sandy nodded.

They were emerging from the brief countryside now, and approaching the new housing estates which marked the extent to which Kirkcaldy was growing. In a few years, Sandy saw, Carsden would be merely a part of Kirkcaldy, rather than being, as his Geography teacher had put it, a dormitory town. The old man with the nodding head looked at all the white houses where fields had once been. His lips puckered into a wet, creased O. He pointed towards the houses. He was mumbling to himself, ignored by everyone. Sandy knew that people were naive. They would not accept what was happening in the world. Yet, in a way, they were responsible. No, that was not correct. People elsewhere, far, far away from Carsden and these new houses, were to blame. They it was who pushed the town's boundary out a few more feet. They were to blame, yet Sandy did not know even who 'they' were.

He nodded his head. He would be old himself one day, but he would not be as stupid as the old man in front of him. He watched from his window as Kirkcaldy grew before him, exhibiting itself to him proudly. It seemed at once malevolent and strange. There were places here in which to get hopelessly lost. There were gangs here more vicious than any in Carsden. There were tower-blocks and a dark, foaming sea and thousands of people, people whose home he was now invading. Having passed the Georgian houses which sat uneasily around the postwar shopping centre, from the top deck of the bus Sandy could see the sea, the North Sea, in its dark grey covering. Even today, with the sun high above it, the sea remained a grizzled colour of the past. The occupants of the bus were excited now. The old people fretted to get their bags ready, keen to be seen not to be dilatory. Young families shouted at one another. The husband would clasp his cigarette between his teeth and wrestle with the youngest child while the mother pushed around the other children and caused them to scream harder. Mark and Clark hovered above their seats, squinting towards the shops and the Saturday crowd.

'What's the plan then?' asked Colin, sensibly.

'Record shops,' said Clark.

'And the pub,' said Mark.

They all looked at Sandy for his suggestion. He was still horrified by the squabble in front of him. The old man was tottering towards the stairs. What if the bus toppled over? Then all these people would fall over one another, smothering in a jellied mass of flailing and crying. Horrible. He would smash the back window quickly and crawl out. He would bring help. He looked towards his expectant friends.

'What's it to be then, Sandy?'

'The sea,' he said, wiping sweat from his forehead. 'The sea.'

They laughed and slapped him and thought that he was joking.

Andy Wallace revved the car once, turned off the ignition, leapt out, and opened the squeaking gate to Mary Miller's house. He had brought along a travelling rug, he told her, in case they took a picnic with them. Mary thought it a good idea. She found some meat spread and cheese and made up some sandwiches while Andy fingered the many ornaments in the living room. Most of these ornaments were either Mary's mother's or else her grandmother's. What others there were had been bought for Mary's birthdays and Christmases by Sandy when a small boy. Andy loathed the tiny ornaments, mostly cheap reproductions, which were to be found crammed into many of the houses, working-class and middle-class, in this part of Fife. He felt they were like useless fancy goods shops – the garish reminders of holidays and the stupid little animals were everywhere. They were part of the sham life that had nothing to do with the realities of the situation. Still, he quite liked Mary's ornaments: for one thing they were Mary's, and for another they were mostly rare, original pieces (apart from Sandy's additions, which were easily discerned). They were also tasteful. He played with a paperweight. It was heavy, and made a satisfying slap in his palm when he tossed it and caught it. This was his kind of ornament.

Mary put everything in a cake tin: sandwiches already wrapped, some biscuits, two hard-boiled eggs, napkins, salt, pepper, a knife. She filled a flask with coffee and milk. Andy came through as she was pouring the water in, thinking to herself of the times when she had, as a youngster, filled her hot-water bottle on cold nights, the task overseen by her mother. Andy said that he had a bottle of wine in his car. Mary brought two glasses out of a cupboard and wiped them. Did he have a corkscrew? He did. She pecked his cheek. He informed her that he also had two crystal glasses in the car. They both smiled. He continued to smile. After a picnic and some wine, lying on a tartan rug in some distant, deserted field, who could refuse him his request?

*

Mark laughed. He had stolen some cut-price singles from the counter of a small record shop and had not been caught. He fanned them out and laughed. The others smiled nervously. Sandy dared to look behind them as they walked, just to make sure. They would try to get into the afternoon's X-certificate offering at the ABC, but first they would eat pie and chips from a baker's shop, then would have a quick pint each at the Harbour Tavern. They were walking now from one end of the High Street to the other, dodging the frazzled shoppers. They glowered at other gangs of four or less, who looked just like them. They grinned at girls their age in tight jeans and budding T-shirts. Clark whistled loudly through the window of a shop to the young girl behind the counter therein. Sandy sang a pop song, allowing his voice to become louder than usual. The shoppers looked at him askance, and he hardly even blushed. They were having a good afternoon. It was Saturday. It was being alive.

When they reached the Harbour Tavern, having noisily consumed their greasy lunch while taking a slight detour down to the esplanade, Colin was the brave one who went through the chipped wooden door first and into the smoke and beer and the noise of the television. Sandy held back. He had seen something. Near the Harbour Tavern, on the other side of the road, was a snooker hall above an amusement arcade. Robbie was speaking to Rian outside the entrance to the snooker hall. It was the first time, Sandy realised, that he had seen either of them outside of the grounds of the mansion. They looked strange, incongruous, as though something only dreamt had suddenly appeared in real life. Sandy watched as Robbie entered the hall, cue in a bashed case tucked beneath his arm. Rian looked at her feet, then sat on the front step of the hall. She rested her head on her hands and watched people walking past eating chips and other vinegary foods. Sandy realised that she was hungry. He felt guilty. His heart pounded. The money felt heavy in his pocket. Yet he did not want his friends to know about Rian. Hearing them call from inside, he pushed open the door. Rian looked across towards him, and he quickly closed the door behind him.

Four men played pool in the middle of the pub and swore at each other. They were vivacious, and they were practically the only people in the bar. A jukebox fought with the volume of the television, from where a racing commentator tipped his hat towards Sandy and murmured something about the afternoon's racing. Sandy looked for a clock. It was one twenty. His friends were being served with beer at the bar. The barman was courteous, knowing that they were all underage. They walked timidly, but pleased, with their drinks over to a corner table. Colin picked up a newspaper lying there and began to read nonchalantly. Mark and Clark gulped their drinks greedily and looked about them, examining the bar's interior like pioneers in a new continent. Sandy, last served, was wondering what to do. He had not seen Rian for some time. He wanted to see her, especially when Robbie was elsewhere, but how could he get away from his friends? He sat down at the table. It had not been wiped recently, if at all in living memory. Rings cut into more rings, the whole becoming a complex, interlinked artwork. Sandy made several more marks with the bottom of his own glass. His mother, when baking, cut out circles of pastry with the rim of a cup. He ran his finger around the rim of his cold, wet glass. Mark and Clark spoke in hushed, respectful tones. They watched the men playing pool, but not too closely.

'The film starts in twenty minutes,' said Sandy, having taken a long draw on his drink and consequently feeling gassy and sick. 'There's something I really have to do before then. I'll leave you here and meet you at the ABC. Is that okay?' They looked at him.

'Scaredy-cat,' said Clark.

Colin rubbed at his face, touching lightly the landscape of acne around his mouth.

'Fine then,' he said, reaching the same hand for his drink. 'See you.'

'Who wants this?' said Sandy, pointing to his glass as he rose. There were three takers. He walked back into piercing daylight and fresh air. She had flown from her perch. Shit. He crossed the road quickly, hearing change jangling in his pocket. Perhaps she had gone off begging for money for food. He had money he could give her. He opened the door of the snooker hall, climbed the stairs, and stared through the glass into the hall itself. There was Robbie, playing by himself and cursing a bad shot, then looking slyly around at the other players. There was no sign of Rian. Sandy ran back down the stairs two at a time and opened the door. He looked left and right. There were so many people milling around, presenting him with a constantly slow-moving obstacle. He walked back along the High Street, looking in shops and crossing the road often to maximise his search. People were already queuing for the film. He did not have much time. Where was she? He remembered her kisses. He could hardly recall her face, but he knew her kisses as he had once known his mother's nipple. Both were sustaining forces. He clung to images of Rian and felt his shirt sticking to his back as he ran.

At the other end of the High Street he cursed the emptiness of his search. He decided to cut down on to the esplanade. Yes, if she were waiting for Robbie that would be as nice a place to wait as any. He found a narrow close between two shops and began to hurry down it, realising almost immediately that, as if in a dream, Rian was walking towards him from a long way away, her eyes on the ground, her legs weary. A man was walking the other way, down towards the esplanade. Sandy stopped. Rian looked up. Her face was red, her mouth redder than the rest. She was flustered by his sudden appearance, as he was by hers. They stood some feet apart, Sandy dripping sweat and breathing heavily.

'Rian?' he said, taking a step closer. Then he looked past her to where the man had been. 'What are you doing?' She became a bad actress.

'Oh, I've just been walking. Waiting for Robbie. He's playing snooker. Losing money probably. I'm just . . .' She smiled at him. Her eyes were slightly wet, shell-like, as if the tide had touched them some time before. 'Let's walk,' she said, taking his arm. 'What are you doing here? You've been running. Did I see you going into a pub near the snooker hall?' She moved him away with her towards the High Street. Sandy panicked. He did not want to go back up there, back where all the people, all the potential enemies were, where his friends might see him with her. He tugged her arm.

'No,' he said, 'this way,' and she, compliant, let herself be taken down to the sea.

They sat on a hillside, sheltered by a boulder which made an excellent windbreak, and talked and laughed and ate and drank. Mary felt happier than she had done in some time. She looked at her 'young man', as she called him, and was happy. He was the perfect gentleman. He served the wine and told her funny stories about school. He acted one of them out for her. She choked on her drink and got hiccups which took some time to dispel. The wine was finished. He let her in on a little secret. He had another bottle in the car. He winked and trotted downhill to fetch it. Mary stifled her hiccups and tried to think straight. She was getting drunk. She focused on the landscape. From her position on the side of a sloping hill she could see Loch Leven in the distance. Tiny boats bobbed on the still surface of the loch, doubtless fishing. Kinross was even further away. They were going to Kinross for an evening meal, though she had said nothing to Sandy about being back late. Andy had told her that she needed to enjoy herself for a change. Rashly, she had agreed with him. She heard him singing as he clambered back towards her, his eyes alight and a bottle swinging from one hand.

They ate bananas and grapes while they sat on the sea-wall. The tide was out. An ominous trawler sat a good way out in the steel-coloured water. Sandy wanted to ask her about the man, but could not force himself to speak the words. They spoke instead of more banal matters. Her voice was a soft, living thing, something that might be found on a beach as the tide was turning. Something no one would take home with them because to do so would be to destroy it for ever. She spoke to him of her youth and her childhood and the few remembrances she had of when she had still been a baby. Sandy could remember nothing as far back as that. Ah, she told him, it was a special gift. She could remember her aunt lifting her to her breast and holding her face to that suffocating dull thing for a long time, longer than a feeding time. It might have been days. Sandy blushed at this image. He looked at her casually, but her face was innocence. She spoke on. The first time she had seen Robbie drunk. The first time she had been sent to beg for money. The time they had moved to the mansion. All the times. The sun was coming down low over them, curving down from its once great height until it swathed them in gold. Sandy thought that it must be getting late. Finally Rian coughed and said, 'Sandy, I've got to tell you. Promise you won't say anything. Promise.' Her insistent eyes made him nod his head. She lowered her eyes then and spoke on, while gulls played on the seashore and a small boy poked with a stick at shadowy things by the water-line.

'I told you that you must trust me and not believe anything Robbie tells you. You've got to believe what I'm telling you now. Robbie is fed up with me. He's fed up of having to go out begging. He knows that it's me that brings in the money anyway. He's started to sell me, Sandy.' Her voice faded to nothing for a second. She coughed again, swallowed, and continued. 'I've got to do things for money, you know, with men. Nothing really serious. But it's horrible.' Her voice became a whisper, like a ghost in his burning ear. 'Robbie makes me give him the money. It saves him having to do any work himself, you see. That man in the alley . . . You almost . . . Well, you know.'

I don't really know, Rian, he wanted to say. Tell me. Tell me. He was ashamed of his grown erection, but there was disgust in his heart. Beer and pie and fruit churned uneasily in his stomach.

'It's not anything too serious yet, but I'm afraid. We had to leave the camp, you know. It was because our Auntie Kitty wanted to use me for much the same thing, I think. I'm not sure now. But Robbie still goes to see her. I think she's poisoned his mind against me. Oh, Sandy . . .' Tears glimmered in her lashes, but would not fall. 'I don't know what to do. Robbie's all I've got. Don't tell him I told you. Please don't. But I had to tell you. I had to. I love you, Sandy.' She looked at him and sniffled.

Sandy was staring hard at the beach where two

gulls fought over a scrap of food. He was thinking back to his evenings in the mansion. It did not seem to fit. Hadn't Robbie been the one who looked scared? Hadn't Rian seemed the strong one? Robbie had been quite good to him, had said things. He could not think straight. Sandy thought that it must be after five. The film would be coming out. He had to catch the bus. His mother. His friends. What about Robbie?

'What about Robbie?' he said.

'What time is it?' she asked. He shrugged his shoulders. Easily, she slid from the sea-wall and walked coyly over to a strolling man, who told her the time with a leer. Sandy examined her, this girlfriend of his. He realised that he had not the power to make her truly his, that any decision would be hers and hers alone. He shrugged off the knowledge, but felt wounded by it all the same.

'It's just five o'clock,' she said. 'I suppose I should go and get Robbie.'

They walked along the esplanade together, their bodies about a foot apart, their arms dangling close to each other. They spoke little. He left her near the snooker hall and walked back along the esplanade towards the bus stop. He went into an amusement arcade and was asked by the proprietor if he could prove his age.

'I'm just past eighteen,' he protested.

'Well, you don't look it, son. If you don't have any means of proving your age then you'll have to go.'

'But I got served at the Harbour Tavern!'

He found himself astonished and back on the

pavement. Seagulls laughed overhead. He glared at them as they swerved high in their inviolable space. He would build wings and swoop up beside them, grabbing with nimble hands and throttling them into his sack. Nobody would laugh at him then.

Colin, Clark and Mark were unmistakable, even against the low and orange sun. They were coming down from the High Street like spent gunslingers. Sandy walked towards them.

'Hello, Sandy. What was the film like?' asked Colin before Sandy could ask him the same question. 'Did you get in?' It took a second for the truth to dawn on Sandy.

'Of course I did,' he said. 'Where were you lot?'

'We didn't get in. Not old enough,' said Colin, while Mark and Clark asked Sandy for details. The four young boys, nearly men but not quite accepted as such, walked with hands in pockets towards a revving bus, Sandy lying to his friends gloriously about a film he had just not seen.

'I'm sorry,' said Mary. She was sobbing. Her blouse was disarranged. She plucked fibres of wool out of the travel-rug. Andy rubbed his hair, scratching at the scalp. He sighed.

'No, *I'm* sorry, Mary,' he said. 'I shouldn't even have tried. I apologise. I don't know . . . the wine and everything. I just felt, well, I'm sorry.'

Mary's sobbing increased. She shook her head violently. 'No, no, no,' she said, 'it's not you. It's me. *Me*. I'm to blame. But you've got to listen to me,

Andy. I don't want to talk about it, but you must listen.'

Andy lay back. The sun was low over the hills. They seemed so very far away from everyone and everything. Yet it had not happened. He had planned it all to perfection, but Mary had not allowed it to happen. He felt embarrassment more than anything else. He had timed everything so well. The second bottle of wine had been finished. Mary had been lying on her back with her eyes closed. A light breeze had curled around the rock, wafting over her face, drawing fine strands of silver hair across her eyes. Andy had bent low over her and kissed her neck, then her chin, then her ready mouth. He had slid down beside her and held her in his arms. Finally, and a long time later it was, she had panicked and pushed him away, gasping. She had sat upright and rigid. She had begun to weep.

Now she summoned up the courage to speak.

'Andy,' she said, 'I've not slept with a man for over sixteen years.' She was still pulling fibres out of the travel-rug. Andy watched her fingers as they slashed at the wool. 'In fact, since the night . . . the night Sandy was . . . was conceived. I've slept with no man since that night.' She looked up at him. Her eyes were difficult to interpret, melting yet defiant. 'I'm frightened, that's all. I need time. Please give me time.' These words were evenly spaced by slight pauses, as if she were rehearsing a speech. Andy's eyes were on hers as she spoke, but she closed her eyes suddenly as if fatigued. A single tear pushed from her eye like a chick escaping from its shell and wriggled its way down her cheek.

'Do you want to talk about it?' he asked softly. She shook her head. He wanted to press the point, but could not. She lay in his arms and slumbered until the sun fell away from the earth and the evening grew too cool for human sleep. It was time to return home.

9

The elderly man, hands dumped in his pockets as if stitched to the material, spat on to his favourite spot of pavement and watched the boy through slanted eyes. He had just left the bookmaker's, having lost a couple of crucial pounds, and was now, in his eternal bitterness, confronted by the memory of his only son's tragic death. He watched closely as the boy jauntily walked down from the direction of Cardell towards him. He curved his hands into taut fists. He was old perhaps, but there was strength in his heart for hatred, and hatred was what he felt for the boy and the whore of a witch who was his mother.

Sandy came to the low wall around one of the elderly persons' bungalows. He hoisted himself on to it and, dangling his legs, thought about Rian and her cryptic words to him. Could he believe her? And if he did, what more was she hiding from him?

The sun was shining again, and there was even sceptical talk in the town of a drought. Sandy looked across the road to where the fruit shop sat. He had no money today for fruit. A small foreign car slowed as it near him. It stopped. The window was rolled down slowly and a voice called him over to the car.

A bearded but young man craned his head out of the window as far as his seat-belt would allow. His blue eyes glistened. Sandy could not meet their intensity. He looked casually off into the distance as he crouched beside the yellow car. He saw an old man's figure hunched outside the betting shop. He knew who that man was. His eyes found their only shelter on the mottled tarmac of the pavement.

'Sorry,' the man was saying, 'but I'm trying to find St Cuthbert's Parish Church. I think these instructions must be wrong.' He rustled a piece of paper on which were drawn several black lines. His voice was Scottish, but never Fife. He was certainly educated. He sounded like a television presenter. 'I've been there before, but I'm afraid my sense of direction must be hopeless.' Sandy nodded and creased his brow.

'Well,' he said slowly, 'you've got to go back the way you just came, but then turn left over the bridge.' The man nodded. He had come from the right, from central Fife, from further afield, from Edinburgh perhaps.

'Thank you very much,' the man said. 'I'm to be the new minister here, God and the people willing. Can I expect to see you and your parents at church some day?'

Sandy stared at him. The cheek of the man! He was grinning through his beard, and Sandy creased his own mouth wryly.

'Some day,' he said. 'Some day.' The minister laughed. It was a great big open natural sound. Sandy liked the new minister so far. The window was rolled up. The car drew away, did a quick three-point turn, and, with a toot of its horn, a toot Sandy acknowledged with a casual wave, made off. Sandy had decided to ignore the old man. Let him stare. He had as much right to be here as anyone.

Matt Duncan spat again. He had been in this town for sixty years. Was he not the man to ask directions off? But no, someone had stopped and asked the dirty black little upstart. Well let them, and let everyone forget about his son Matty. Let the town forget that tragedy; the wickedness of the witch. He would never forget. He forged horseshoes made of fire in his heart. There could be no forgetting. His son had died by fire. Now fire burned within the father. Let them all forget. But before he, Matt Duncan, died, there would be a reckoning. He screwed up his eyes until only a thin sliver of vision remained. In this sliver, the boy, seated again on his wall, became a blurred thing, a crouched goblin, the spawn of a witch, something insignificant which Matt Duncan would have squashed with a hardened and unfeeling palm as if eradicating a sin.

There were some little notebooks in a cupboard, and inside these discoloured relics, in the tiniest, neatest script, her grandmother had written down recipes for certain herbal curatives. This, to Mary's knowledge, was as close as her grandmother had ever come to witchcraft.

She took the biscuit tin full of notebooks to her bedroom, closed the door properly, and sank on to the bed. She had let herself down. If she was frightened by Andy, gentle Andy, then she was ruined and would be better off dead. She did not seek a poison yet, but was looking for some recipe for the relaxing of women under stress. She knew, in her heart of hearts, that the problem was deeper than could be cured by any drug, yet she had to try, had to do something. Else she would go off her head. For Sandy's sake, she could not do that yet. Sandy. Sandy. He was her life's work, her everything. If only he was a little older. He seemed in a limbo: still tied to school, and yet not doing anything with his remaining time there. He was at an age that was no age. She wished she could help him, but then who was she to help anybody? She leafed through the fragile books, but found the writing difficult. Photographs showed that her grandmother had been a tiny creature with a pointed, puckered face and childish hands. White strands of hair flaked loose from her bun. She looked comical, ancient and wise. Sandy used to marvel that, to an extent, he was her kin. He would study her photographs for hours when a child, asking his mother and grandmother impossible questions as to identities of people and places. The album of loose photographs was now left untouched, and only seldom added to, such as in the period immediately after she had given Sandy a camera for his eleventh birthday. Photographs were memories of happy times. Perhaps that was why the album had become so little used. Ever since . . . Oh, she could burst that knowledge from her mouth! It was intolerable. Sandy, Sandy, Sandy, why have you never asked who your father was? Why? And why had she kept it bottled up all those years to have doubt and rumour still cast upon her?

She put a notebook to her nose and, sniffing its powerful smell, closed her eyes to let the weeping begin. She sat there, convulsed, and allowed her tears to drop noisily into the biscuit tin, splashing the ancient mementoes within.

The Reverend Iain J. M. Darroch, MA, BD, looked around his new church. It was a dull, dreary old building, smelling of polished pews and damp rafters. The only ornamentation came from the brass rails, the stained-glass depiction of Christ, and the empty vases on the window sills. He paced the floor between the aisles. He had been driven here for a preliminary look at the place a few days before, but had not really been looking at all. He looked now, though. A regular congregation of one hundred and thirty. One hundred communicants. It was dreary, but then he liked the prospect of a challenge, after the stuffiness of the degree itself and the nightmare time he had spent in the Oxgangs district of Edinburgh as an assistant. That had been a terrible year, a year which had cast doubt on his abilities. But here he was: his first full parish, if he were accepted. Things could only get better.

Mr Ancram, the elder he had met on his first visit, came into the church through the small door beside the pulpit. He greeted the young minister cordially, apologising for not having been present on his arrival. Did he wish to go across to the manse? Did he have his things with him? Iain Darroch replied that the car was pretty full, and that a furniture van would be bringing the bulk of his possessions in a few hours' time. Mr Ancram nodded. Mr Ancram and two other members of the Vacancy Committee had been to see the Reverend Darroch preaching at Oxgangs on the previous Sunday. All three thought that there would be no problem regarding his acceptance by their congregation. The minister looked around his new church one last time. He knew that his first sermon would have to be stimulating, or else he would soon lose his parishioners and his congregation. They feared young ministers around here, the minister of nearby Cardell Parish Church had written to inform him. He hoped to meet with that minister, the Reverend Walker, soon. But first he would have to get settled in and finish the inaugural sermon, which he had been preparing for the past three days. He would lose no kirkgoer without a fight. And he would succeed, with God's grace.

Iain Darroch had been born in the East Neuk of Fife, the nose of the Scottie dog when Fife is examined on a map. Crail had been a quiet fishing port, more a tourist spot than an actual working harbour, though once it had been industrious and important. As a child, he had been uninterested in the quayside, in the lobster creels and their dark snapping catches. He had been a bookworm; not enough in the sun, his parents contended. They might well have been right. He was now pallid and skinny. The beard had been grown to hide his sallow face, but still it could be seen in his watery eyes. His mother had been proud of his intention to become a minister. His father had been surprised, but had said little. So, without much of the congratulation which the boy had assumed would be his, he had entered the local university of St Andrews, going on to do his Divinity degree at Edinburgh. This was his end. A town in Fife, more dead than alive. Not one of the East Neuk's prosperous and civilised villages, but a redundant mining town, a town where God was needed, but was perhaps so seemingly absent as to have been rejected altogether by the majority of the inhabitants. Yet the town boasted two kirks – his own (his *own*!) and Reverend Walker's. He hoped that there would be no poaching, then rebuked himself to the cloudless sky.

'Couldn't have asked for a nicer day,' said Mr Ancram.

'Very true,' said Iain Darroch. He crossed the busy road. 'Where does this road go?' he asked.

'Kirkcaldy that way,' said the elder, 'and Lochgelly the other. Which way did you come in?'

'I think I misread my directions. I came in through Lochgelly, but then ended up coming through Dundell.'

'Yes, that's a long road round all right. Still, it's the only way to find your way around, isn't it?'

'True, very true.' Iain Darroch was aware that, in his attempt to impress Mr Ancram, he was sounding boringly ministerial, very self-righteous. He sounded like his minister at Oxgangs. He rebuked himself again for that cruel thought. The Devil was afoot today.

The manse was a small detached house. 'Used to belong to one of the pits,' explained Mr Ancram. 'One of the foremen or something used to stay in it. Belonged to St Cuthbert's since about 1965, I suppose. A nice little place. Maybe a bit roomy for a bachelor. The Reverend Davidson and his poor wife liked it well enough.'

Ancram looked at him. It was the first hint. They liked their ministers to be married, thought Darroch. He said, 'Yes, I saw it when I was here on Monday. Do you remember? Yes, it is a nice house.'

Mr Ancram opened the door with a small batch of keys, then handed the whole bunch to the minister. 'All yours, Mr Darroch. You'll find out what they're for.' He smiled. The minister smiled back. He felt thankful for his beard. It could be used as a defence against the outside world. He hid behind it now as one would have hidden behind a clump of gorse. He entered his home, his new home. It smelled of past occupants. He blessed it silently when he entered, hoping that the past occupants would take the hint and skedaddle with their aromas of old beds and polished dressers. He opened the doors and some of the windows that would actually open. He looked in drawers and cupboards and was pleased to find that, as promised, the house boasted sufficient linen, cutlery and crockery for his immediate needs. He brought in some of the boxes from his car, aided by Mr Ancram. From the first of these he took an electric kettle. He let the tap in the kitchen run for a full minute, then filled the kettle and plugged it in to a handy socket. From the same box he took a jar of coffee and a plastic container of dried milk. Mr Ancram came in from the toilet, shaking his hands to show, perhaps, that he had washed them.

'A cup of coffee, Mr Ancram?' asked Darroch, proud of his efficiency in the matter. Mr Ancram shook his head, still wafting his hands.

'I don't drink the stuff,' he informed the minister. 'It is an irritant.' Darroch looked at the man, making a mental note that Mr Ancram had not yet invited the new minister to address him by his Christian name, whatever that might be. Mr Ancram looked at his watch. 'Actually, I'd better be off,' he said. 'I've to pick up my wife from the supermarket in Kirkcaldy. She's doing the month's shopping.' Darroch nodded, spooning one of milk and two of coffee (just to spite the man) into a cup. 'I'm sorry I won't be here to help you move in the rest of your belongings,' Mr Ancram apologised. 'I'll drop round later and see how you're managing. Bye now.'

'Goodbye, Mr Ancram,' said Darroch, 'and thanks for your help.' He ignored the man's exit and rummaged in another, smaller box until he found the packet of cream biscuits. He smiled to himself. Luxury. He went through to the living room and sat in the large fireside chair. A wind was blowing through the open window. It was a good breeze. Darroch sat and drank his coffee. It was far too strong. He considered his new surroundings. It did not really matter where he was – Crail, Oxgangs, Carsden – the situation and the realities were the same. The Church was in a state of acute decay, which seemed to run hand in hand with the decay of the communities. Which came first? Did either? It seemed to him that a larger, much more potent force was at work, and it was a force of evil. He could not feel God in this town. It would be his job to bring God back to these people, who were more walking shadows than real flesh and blood. The Church had become lazy. Aching gashes had opened up which now needed filling. God, let him do his job well enough. He sucked crumbs from his fingers and prayed.

Every summer, Andy Wallace began reading Cervantes' *Don Quixote*, and every summer he failed to finish it. He saw no reason why this summer should be any different. He had been reading the book for about three hours when he felt his eyes and his mind falling from the page. He read two pages more, but could not, having read them, remember the slightest detail of their content. He put the book down and sat staring into space. He was thinking about Mary. He was thinking about the problem he must help her surmount. There were sex manuals in his house, little more than masturbation fodder, but he had reread them anyway. They threw little light on the dilemma. He sat in his study, which had now become almost his whole existence. He had work to do. Apart from the Cervantes book, there were exercises to be set, essays and exam papers to be marked, and the part-completed novel which had been sitting untouched in a drawer for three months. It was a bad novel, amateurish, but just to finish it would be achievement enough, even if it was the worst novel in the world, read by no one save himself. He had given it none of his time since he had begun to see Mary. She was still on his mind. That Saturday afternoon on the hillside played again and again like a bad song on popular radio. He caught its melody again and again. There was no escape. What to do about Mary. Mary, Mary, quite contrary, how does your garden grow? He shook his head clear of the reverie and sat down at his desk. He removed the lid from the typewriter. He began to type his thoughts down on to the black rubber carriage. He could see the ink wet and bluey-black against the fainter black. He pressed his finger to a word and examined the imprint. Mirror writing. He smudged it, wetted the finger, and the word vanished completely. It was as easy as that on a typewriter carriage.

Dear Mary,

Yes, it's that time again – a letter from your ageing brother. How's tricks? How's life with old Andy Schoolmaster? I hope he's treating you in the style to which etc etc. And how is my little Sandy? His exams must be long over by now (?). I hope he's enjoying his vacation. I'm planning on going north to the wilder parts of this fine country in a few weeks. Tell him that he doesn't know what he's missing, not coming across to see his long-lost Unc. I see from a recent correspondence with my bank manager and yours that you haven't touched the account yet. Like I said, sis, I'm not touching it, so it's all yours. Should you need it. I know that I bring this up every letter, but it is important to me.

*Okay? Looks like I'm being shifted to our Toronto office.
I don't know what this means. I think it probably
means that Old Emerson has got tired of having
someone efficient and trustworthy around here. Still,
joking apart, it means I'm in with the really big boys
(oh goody-goody!). I'm earning so much it's embarrassing. In fact, I'm earning so much I can afford to take a
girl out every now and again. I've been seeing quite a
few ladies recently, one of whom I can even stand.
Maybe things are looking up. (There might be a bad
joke hidden in there somewhere, but I'm not saying
where.)*

*Well, Mary, I've not written a very long letter, but I
know that you will, as always, understand. I get very
little time to myself these days. It's all company this and
company that, not forgetting female company. God, if I
got the boot from Emerson maybe I could make it as a
professional comedian. What do you say? Listen, tell
Sandy he gets no Christmas pressie this year if he
doesn't put pen to paper pronto and write to Santa
Tom. Okay? The office beckons. Och aye the noo. Take
best care.*

Tom
xxx

10

She was drowning. There were weeds above and around her. They twisted themselves sinuously around her arms and legs, embracing her. She could not find the bottom. There was no bottom. Bubbles of precious air escaped from her nostrils. Her lungs ached. Her brain told her one thing, but her heart was telling her another. Eventually her heart won. She opened her mouth and felt the water gushing in. The choking commenced. Her eyes began to darken. Then the pain hit her, centred in her head, right at the scalp. She began painfully to rise towards what looked like the surface. She was a long way beneath the glittering pool of light, but slowly she floated towards it. She broke the surface with a choke from her mouth and water dribbling down her chin, as if she were some badly fed baby. She roared. The pain was in her stomach now, as if her belly was distending with some quickening foetus. She wiped her face and cried out at the injustice. Andy was there to comfort her. Some of her hair had come out at the roots and he wiped it from his hands. He settled her back on the wet grass. Her dress was clinging to her. She was almost naked. Her body was clearly visible through the saturated cotton, as if she were a dancer behind the silkiest of veils. She lay back to rest, but Andy's fingers were touching her. He was towering over her. He was speaking, but the water still rushed in her ears. The word she could make out was 'reward'. He was tugging at her dress, lying across her now. All at once she realised what he was about to do. She pushed at him, her arms weak. She wanted to tell him that she was already pregnant. She tried to shout, but only water gurgled from her throat. She had become a fish, flailing on land, the line still holding her. She gurgled in protest. There was a shadowy figure behind Andy now. Then two shadowy figures, watching interestedly, their hands behind their backs. She beat at Andy with her fists. She cleared the water from her lungs and screamed . . .

The pillow was over her head. She shook herself free of it, drew back the bedcovers, and sat up. She was damp with sweat. It was light behind the blue curtains. She fumbled for the clock, brought it to her, and found that it was five thirty. The birds were singing outside. What a nightmare. She shook her hair, crumpling it into place. Patting the sheets, she found that she had wet the bed.

She rose quickly, put on her slippers, and stripped off the sheet. She tucked it under her arm and padded down to the kitchen, avoiding the creaky parts of the staircase for fear of waking Sandy. In the kitchen she stuffed the sheet into her washing basket, filled the kettle, plugged it in, and slumped on to one of the stools.

She had very occasionally, in the past twenty

years, dreamt of drowning, of that day in the hot burn, but never had Andy been a part of the dream before, and never had she wet the bed. The reason why Andy now entered the dream was crystal clear to her. She felt like crying, but the kettle had boiled, so she made the tea and, feeling that this was breakfast-time, buttered some bread which she then cut into half-slice triangles. She stirred a spoonful of sugar into her tea. She tried to persuade herself that it would take time, this curative. With Andy's patience she would win through. She hoped that she would not need to submit herself to any specialist. She could not tell anyone her horror story. Not even Andy? Not yet anyway. She looked to the ceiling. The paint was cracked from light fitting to back door. It had been like that for years. Sandy was asleep just a few feet above her. She closed her eyes for a moment. No, she did not regret it. Regret lay elsewhere. Regret lay in someone's shame, in someone's eternal shame.

She heard the floorboards creak. Sandy walked slowly to the bathroom. The toilet flushed. He padded back to bed. She sat in silence, comfortable with the secret that she was already awake and up and listening to him.

Sandy, having wiped himself with toilet paper, returned to his bed and tried to avoid the chilled, clammy patch on his sheet. He had not experienced a wet dream for a long time. He tried to get to sleep again, to perhaps take up the dream, but could not. He listened to the silence of the house. Sometimes he thought that he could hear his mother's breathing. He had been dreaming of Rian, naturally. She had been walking naked through the mansion, touching things. He had watched her, nothing more. Just her nakedness had brought him beyond. The cold patch of wet had rung like an alarm clock and brought his dream to an inconclusive end. He could not recall at what point exactly in the dream he had come. That was unusual. He wanted Rian more badly than ever. He wanted to walk up Main Street with her, his arm over her shoulders, and show everyone, all the gossipy old women and the unemployed men and the gangs of young boys, that she was his, only his. But these stories she told: could they be true, and if they were, then what exactly did she do for these men? And for Robbie, come to that. Sandy knew that he could not beat Robbie in a fair fight. What he could do was take Rian away from him by stealth and bring her here to stay with his mother and him. It was the wildest of plans. It was the only plan he had. How could he ask his mother? Would she understand? Surely, once he had put the facts to her, she could not refuse. She, more than anyone, knew what it was like to be an outsider, to be cast out and have to depend on yourself. He would put it to her that Rian was in the same situation. A refugee of sorts. He would ask her, but first he had to see Rian. And he had to find out the truth, which meant talking with Robbie when Rian was not present. He had much to do. A trickle of watery semen escaped and ran coolly down his thigh. He rubbed it dry and hoped that the sheet wouldn't stain.

Mary, tidying his room later that day while Sandy was out (he hated her doing this, feeling that it breached his privacy), found the hardened patch on the white sheet. She smiled a little as she tucked in the top sheet and threw the blanket over the bed. It was about time Sandy had a girl of his own, she thought to herself. He was a bit old now for this sort of thing. She caught herself – what was she thinking! The boy was only fifteen, albeit fifteen and ten months. She was his mother after all. The last thing she should want was for him to get some girl into trouble. Nocturnal emissions did no harm. She piled up some pop magazines and put them beside his bed. Then she dusted, spraying polish on to the wooden surfaces. The smell was beautiful. Nothing resembled it. She put the duster to her nose. Beautiful. She hummed a song to herself as she closed the door and went through to her own room. She rarely dusted in the back room.

This afternoon she would visit the grave and tell her mother about the wonderful weather, the ban on hosepipes. Later, Andy was taking her to Kirkcaldy. She had to make out a shopping list, though he would be disappointed that it was not to be a pleasure-only trip. She hoped that Sandy would come along too. There was a tension between Andy and her son, quite understandably, but the only way to break it was for them to meet often and find out about each other. She thought of herself as a humble amateur psychologist and matchmaker as she sprayed her polish liberally on to the pre-war dresser. She worked the polish in slowly, humming a nonsense tune and smiling. The wood became like the surface of a pond and, staring into it, Mary recoiled from the memory of her nightmare. She went giddy and gripped the edge of the dresser until her eyes cleared. She had to sort things out. She had to. This was something she could not talk to her mother about, not with her father listening. And she could never be certain that he wasn't. Especially today, when she had Tom's letter to tell them about. Her father was bound to be there today. Her speech was nervous when she thought her father might be listening. The man who had killed himself. She was sure it had been suicide. God save him. Dear Lord God save him. She began dusting again. Suicide, because of her.

There was a new minister in town, it was said. It had not taken long. Out with the old and in with the new, with no respectful period of mourning. She would have expected better from the Church. She would go to kirk this week and see what he was like. She doubted if she would like him nearly as well as she had liked the Reverend Davidson. Still, she had to give the man a chance. Everyone warranted a chance.

And perhaps, just perhaps, she would find that she could talk to him.

11

The single bell of St Cuthbert's Parish Church pealed out across the sleeping rooftops of the hungover houses in its midst. The Sunday morning had begun with the sluggish movements of the newspaper boys. A few keening dogs had been walked by their listless owners. Birds feasted up and down Main Street on the discarded wrappings of fish and chips from the raucous night before. These gouged balls of paper would be blown by the morning's breeze down Main Street and into the churchyard itself, lying against the dank walls of the church as if listening to a neighbour's argument.

A car would stop occasionally beside the newsagent's for the Sunday paper and the day's ration of cigarettes. A pool of vomit near the door was finally and inexorably trodden into the shop, making its sticky smell obvious to those who had so carefully tried to avoid its presence outside. Old ladies with old hats pinned to their heads, so long unfashionable as to be nearly fashionable again, would mutter dark utterances to the bleary-eyed newsagent before departing with their pandrops towards the church. They would walk the slow length of Main Street commenting upon a full week's gossip, would enter the awkwardly gravelled kirkyard, and would stand outside talking until the chill pushed them into the doorway, where a trim and proper elder stood smiling, hands clasped importantly in front of him. He would offer them a hymnbook as usual, and they would refuse as usual, having possessed their own (they would inform him) since they had first been able to read, and that wasn't yesterday.

The organist, ruddy-cheeked, had chosen his piece and was playing it to the morning chorus of whispers and coughs as the self-conscious congregation settled into the well-worn, comfortable rhythm of Sunday morning. The bell tolled overhead and around them. It was as if the outside world had never been.

When Mary came into his room carrying a cup of tea and two ginger-nuts, Sandy was waking from another tolerable dream – though a kind of nightmare – concerning Rian and himself.

They were being chased by a gang, and had climbed to the top floor of a block of flats in order to escape. They had found one flat open and had swept inside, locking and bolting the door behind them. It had been a nice flat and Rian had immediately made herself at home, trying out the gadgets in the kitchen and turning on television, radio, stereo. He tried to make her see the danger they were in. The door was being pushed at by some vast, faceless force, but she had ignored him. Look, he said, I'm trying to save us. Can't you help? She had come to him, smiling, as distant as ever, had kissed him on the cheek and had placed a bread knife in his hand. Use this, she had said, and kissed him again. He looked at the obscenely serrated edge of the knife. The door opened a fraction, held only by the chain, and a hand crawled round its edge, fiddling with the lock, trying to snap the flimsy chain. Methodically, but hating himself, he had begun to slice at the hand, which he wedged with all his might into the gap in the door so that it could not escape, and suddenly it was an animal, its body its own, belonging to nothing outside of the door. Gashes, but no blood. Screams, but no mouth. It had dropped to the floor in snake-like agony. Rian had come up behind him with a cup of tea. She had tapped him on the back. A cup of tea, Sandy, she had said. A cup of tea.

It was his mother's voice, too sharp to be part of the dream. He blinked open his eyes and brought his head out from beneath the sheet. The light hit him. The curtains had been opened and his mother was standing in her dressing gown with a mug of tea in her hand.

'Cup of tea?' she repeated. He was plunged back into the dream for a moment, and at the same time was aware of an erection beneath the bedclothes. He sat up, concentrating on the tea and the new day, feeling the throb easing.

'Thanks, Mum,' he said. She began to leave the room.

'Don't bother going back to sleep now. There's new bread and jam for breakfast. I forgot to get bacon yesterday.'

He could smell the bread. His erection was dying. Hunger and the need to pee redirected his thoughts.

He swung out of bed and began to dress, sitting on the bed when finished to dip the ginger-nuts in the milky tea and suck the flavour from them. He had no plans for today. Unless his mother had anything arranged, he would go for a walk later and see who was around. Perhaps Colin would be in the park. He would not go to the mansion. He had not the courage yet.

Downstairs, the ritual of Sunday breakfast was waiting like some seldom-visited aunt. On Saturdays he would usually be out of the house before his mother could call him back to eat something. Saturday was the exciting day of the week. Everything else was build-up or anticlimax, but not a minute of Saturday could be wasted. During the weeks prior to the holidays breakfast had been the rush not to be late for school, a hurried, near-involuntary thing. He would cram toast into his mouth while moving from kitchen to bathroom, bathroom to bedroom. Inevitably, along the way his mug of tea and some piece of vital written work would be lost, and a trail of minute crumbs would show the steps taken to locate both.

Sundays, however, were different. On Sunday there was nothing to hurry for, no school to be late for. On Sunday Sandy had to sit through a lengthy interrogation by his mother while she fed him and poured out mug after mug of tea. She would ask him about his week, and they would discuss important things like potential holidays and television and work. He would answer patiently: she deserved nothing less. He could see how much these mornings meant to her. It was as if she were trying to pretend that they were a normal family, cramming all the mundane details of the week into one overlong morning. She seldom complained on those odd Sundays when a game of football took him careering out of the house, slamming the door on breakfast and conversation and her loneliness. Sometimes when he looked at her across the table he would notice something insignificant in itself such as that her hand shook as she poured the tea, or that she seemed tired, or that she had blistered the back of her hand on the iron leaving a raw red scar against the purer white, and on those occasions something would well up in him: pity and love perhaps, but those words were never adequate.

She was his mother, and one day she would die. It was a chilling reality. He fended it off with thoughts of Rian. Perhaps they would marry one day. On this particular Sunday morning his mother seemed sombre, and he contemplated telling her that he had a girlfriend to cheer her up. But having said that, what else could he truthfully tell her? No, he could not yet bring himself to share his secret love with anyone – especially a love so strange and uncertain – and the knowledge of this isolation caused him to fidget in his chair as his mother leaned over the table with her plate of new bread, heat rising from it even in the warmth of the kitchen.

'Are you going to church this morning, Mum?' he asked. She stopped stirring her tea. She contemplated the bread before her.

'I don't know,' she said. 'Yes, I thought I might go along to welcome the new minister. And then I thought I'd go visit your gran.'

'Oh yes?' he said. 'Gran and Grandad?' He was losing himself again, this time to the warm, soft wetness of the bread, the saltiness of the butter, the sweetness of the jam. He sucked on the paste in his mouth for a long time until the blend of flavours was only a memory, then swallowed and drank some tea and bit off another piece to repeat the process.

The longer they sat, the brighter Mary became. Her eyes at last took on a truly living look. Sandy looked at the clock.

'Is it good bread then?' she said. He nodded. She tipped her head a little in agreement. There was a short silence, not uncomfortable. 'And are you still intent on not staying on at school, Sandy?'

His heart sank.

'It's important,' his mother continued. 'With jobs so short these days you've got to get as many qualifications as possible. You listen to some of the men down the street. They'll tell you. They could kick themselves now for not having stuck in at school. They're all on the midden now that the pits have shut and there's nothing else around here except computers and things that they're not trained for. Brains over brawn, Sandy. That's the way of the world. More and more. The world revolves around intelligence. It's the only way you'll escape this place. So you stick in, and if you need any help, well, I'll see what I can do.' She was eating now.

'Yes, Mum.' It was his best defence. After a few

more minutes he looked meaningfully at the wall clock and she caught the trick and followed his eyes.

'My God,' she said. 'I'd better get dressed if I'm going to the kirk. You finish your breakfast.' He was nodding. She rose from the table. 'I'm away upstairs.'

Sandy relaxed when she left the kitchen. He could hear the creaking of the floorboards above him, locating for him his mother's exact whereabouts. He could picture her every action from this succession of sounds: she was searching in her chest of drawers for clean bra, knickers, tights. She was over by the wardrobe, selecting and taking out her dress, hanging it up. She was gathering the lot together and was walking across the hall to the bathroom. In the bathroom she locked the door for some obscure reason of propriety, then took off her dressing gown and her nightdress. She squatted to pee, tore off some paper with which to wipe herself, and flushed the toilet. She stood at the small sink and looked in the mirror while running the water, then gave herself a good wash, water splashing the floor and the toilet seat. She then dressed quickly, zipping things and clipping things. Snap, the door was unlocked and she padded in her tights to the bedroom. She sat down at her dressing table and again wasted a minute staring into her mirror. Perhaps she was examining her hair. This she would then brush, using long, slow strokes. Perhaps she would dab a little make-up on to heighten the colour of her face, would spray a tiny amount of perfume on to her neck and her wrists, shaking the wrists to dry the spray, then would pull her dress on, bring her shoes out from beneath the bed and slip them on to her feet. Now her feet made great tapping noises on the floor, like a carpenter at work on a roof. Sandy's eyes fixed themselves on the kitchen ceiling. A moment of stillness now from upstairs, a moment he could never explain, then she was descending with her coat over her arm. He rose from the table.

'Your tea's getting cold,' she said. Sandy took her coat from her and helped her into it. She thanked him. 'Quite the gentleman this morning,' she said, smiling, though he did it every time she went to church. 'Not that you're keen to see me go or anything.' She checked in her clutch-purse. 'Right.' She looked around her. 'I've got my key, so if you're going out, lock the door. And please wash the dishes, all right?' He nodded. 'See you later.' She bent down and he offered his cheek to her kiss. Perfume surrounded him, embraced him with its curious strengths. He was smiling all the time. She looked so different when dressed up: so cultured, so other-worldly. She might be beautiful. Sandy had a guilty peek at her legs as she walked to the front door. The boys at school had said that she was a bit of a ride, so she might well be beautiful too.

Iain Darroch stood in his puffed vestments and welcomed his congregation one by one at the porch. Some of the older ones looked him over obtrusively, as if they were planning to buy him like beef at market. Many, indeed, had come solely to inspect the new minister. Some of the younger women stood together gossiping in the kirkyard. They looked at him occasionally, and straightened their backs when doing so. It was a curious sign, and Darroch, though he had some knowledge of human behaviour behind him, was at a loss as to its meaning. He thought perhaps that they were admiring his stature. He was a good inch over six feet, and his chest and shoulders seemed broader than usual due to the unwieldy amount of cloth over them. His stomach sagged only slightly – unnoticed under the robes in any case.

The little old women in their little old hats had trouble climbing the few steep stone steps to the doorway. They puffed and croaked then extended greetings to him, smiling with rows of stained false teeth. He smiled back. His teeth were, excepting two crown fillings, exclusively his own. He was as afraid of dentists as he was of damnation, sometimes believing them to be one and the same thing. He checked himself, raised his eyes briefly and, he hoped, piously to heaven, and begged forgiveness for the flippancy.

A breeze was blowing cold enough to chill his handshake. The men who shook his hand were members, almost to a man, of the Masonic Lodge. He returned their greetings cordially. The church was filling. He had spent the morning going over his notes one last time. Today he knew that he might have the sympathy vote behind him. The real test would be sustaining the momentum over the next few Sundays. Ideally, he should start off strongly, yet get stronger in the weeks that followed. The butter-flies in his whole trunk danced a fandango. It was like being at the dentist's.

The single bell was pealing, activated by an ingenious electric system. No need for a bell-puller in this day and age, unfortunately. A tall well-dressed woman was now treading carefully over the gravel of the kirkyard in her highish heels. Some of the gossiping parties looked at her and then spoke quietly among themselves. He was struck by her dark features, her air of distance from all around her, her white hair blowing out behind her as she moved into the breeze. She climbed the steps and took his hand.

'Mary Miller,' she said. 'How do you do. We live down by where the colliery used to be, at the foot of Cardell.'

He looked into her eyes. They were hazel, but could almost have been black, hidden as they were under a canopy of darkest eyelash and eyebrow.

'I'm very pleased to meet you, Mrs Miller. My name's Iain Darroch, newly arrived from Edinburgh.' He knew that she had a son. The resemblance between her and the boy of whom he had asked directions was stunning: the same dark aloofness, the same bearing of isolation.

'It's actually Miss Miller, though I don't much go in for titles,' she said, smiling. He blinked. Surely he could not be wrong. Discretion was needed here. He bowed his head slightly, but kept silent, smiling also. The striking woman moved into the church, her heels resounding until they reached the carpeted

162

aisle. Having met with most of the congregation, Iain Darroch slipped around to the back of the church quietly, opened a little door there, and prepared himself for the service. Climbing a few wooden steps, he would come to a small door which would take him into the church proper and only a few steps away from his pulpit. He would walk solemnly to the base of the pulpit, climb the stairs to its small, paunch-high door, push it open, and enter the lap of the Lord God to preach His words. Prior to this, the session clerk would have placed the large, heavy Bible open on the rim of the pulpit. He was waiting now for the clerk to come and collect the Bible. God, please be with me this day as I face my trial by jury. Please don't let me bungle anything or seize up. Please, dear Lord, don't let it be like the dentist's.

'We will now sing hymn number three-nine-six. Hymn three hundred and ninety-six. For those of you with the Revised Hymnary, this can be found in the little pamphlets on the pews. Hymn three-nine-six,

> "The King of Glory standeth
> Beside that heart of sin;
> His mighty voice commandeth
> The raging waves within;
> The floods of deepest anguish
> Roll backwards at His will,
> As o'er the storm ariseth
> His mandate, 'Peace, be still' " . . .

Hymn three-nine-six then.' The organist played the tune while the congregation coughed and turned over the pages of their hymnbooks and pamphlets. Now the organ ceased, and the congregation quietly rose.

The young minister's hearty voice drowned out, to his own ears, much of the muted singing from the pews a dizzy depth beneath him. At the singing of the hymn's second line he saw a few eyes wander from their books towards the dark woman, so erect and contented in her pew. She stood to Darroch's right, alone in one of the side pews. The eyes of some of the women strayed often towards her, and now more than before. The heart of sin. Iain Darroch thought that he knew something now of her son. He knew, moreover, of her isolation, this woman with the eyes of a wounded but indomitable soul. He nearly lost his place in the hymn, but recovered with a quick glance at the next line. The poor woman, and so beautiful. He had wandered into a town of enmity and spitefulness, into a town of age-long memories and the slowest forgiveness. How could he remedy things? And dear Lord, should he even try?

' "To dwell with thee above." '

The organ ground its way to a stop. The organist, a Mr Bogie, had a painful style and was of limited resources. His face was ruddy with piety, and his hands gleamed as though soaped to perfection. The small choir sat down, followed by the rest of the congregation. Iain Darroch began the intimations. It was a long list. This was the social side of the Church of Scotland, the side most people relished so far as he could tell. The Church was for coffee mornings and bazaars and Young Mothers' groups and whist drives and the like. The Church was for a society of coffee-swilling whist-players, no different from those portrayed so keenly in *The Rape of the Lock*, one of Darroch's favourite poems. This was a society, moreover, which held hatred at its core, hate and bitter hypocrisy. There would be some strong sermonising in the next few weeks. Pity welled up in the young man. Who could he ask about Mary Miller? Perhaps he had one ally: the Reverend Walker of Cardell Parish Church. He would invite himself to the older man's manse. He finished the intimations.

'The collection,' he said, 'will now be taken.' The organist began some unassuming dirge. Iain Darroch sat himself down and did some thinking.

He went all the same, drawn by her irresistible magnet. He walked around the perimeter of the mansion, hoping that she would somehow sense his presence and come down from her high prison to see him. He whistled and kicked some stones at imaginary goalposts on the walls of the house. He hacked out interminable thistles with his heel. There was no sign of life around the mansion, only the distant shouts and curses from the golf course.

He suddenly felt very afraid. What was he doing there, and what could he say to Robbie or Rian should he encounter them? He felt like the dog tied up outside the butcher's shop.

He crept away from the house and climbed on to the wall adjoining the field of barley. He looked up at the boarded windows, behind which might lie either his girlfriend or else an empty and moaning puzzle. His girlfriend? The word seemed unfit for their strange, queasy relationship. Internecine was a word he had found quite recently in a novel. He had jotted it down in his list of unusual words and had found its meaning in a dictionary. It seemed to fit his situation. Internecine. It had a vague sound like nectar and intercourse, and like nectarine. Internectarine. He smiled, still looking at the house. He would write a poem and call it 'Internectarine', and it would be about two lovers and a peach. He had only the vaguest idea of how to link the two concepts, but then that hardly mattered in poetry.

He slid from the wall into the crumbly earth of the field. He worked his way around its edge, stroking his face with a ripe and broken beard of barley. He might go to the café if it were open. He had a little money. He could go to the newsagent's. He remembered with guilt that he had not washed the breakfast dishes, such as they were. His mother would be home from church, fresh and humming, in a little while. He jogged to the far wall, climbed over, and ran all the way home.

1985
The Flood

1

Svx

'Come in, come in.'

The Reverend Walker was older than Darroch had imagined. Middle age had waved him goodbye and he was settling into a slow, steady pre-retirement stage. He gestured for the young man to go through to the sitting room, then closed the front door with a nervous cough.

Darroch disliked people's nervous coughs. They made him feel awkward. He studied the elderly man's back. It had been strong and straight once, perhaps as recently as ten years ago. Now, however, it was stooped as if in a constant prayer for forgiveness. Death, Darroch supposed, was a pre-eminent concern of the old. He thought about it himself often enough with just the slightest tingling of foreboding. What price then old age and the clutching of fragile straws?

'Sit yourself down. I'm sorry we've not been able to meet sooner. I've been in hospital for some tests. Gracious, these days there's not a part of the body that's left sacrosanct after a visit to the hospital. These doctors think they know it all. They think they have some kind of divine secular right when it comes to poking and prodding the flesh.' The old man scratched at his rich, whitened hair. 'I don't know,' he said. 'We have much to suffer in the ministry in this age. Wouldn't you agree?' Darroch nodded. 'We have to explain divinity,' continued the minister, 'to people who are more and more susceptible to the apparent truths of science. Joseph Conrad once called science "the sacrosanct fetish". An interesting juxtaposition, but a wise phrase, and he was talking in the earliest years of the century. A wise phrase. Have you read Conrad?'

Darroch was allowed the chance of speaking. He merely shook his head.

'Nor I. I found that quote in a dictionary of quotations. I love reading through books like that. It makes you seem astonishingly well read when you meet anyone.' Reverend Walker giggled like a child. 'I even read dictionaries, you know, and send the editors lists of words that have been missed out. You'd be surprised at the words some dictionaries omit. I think I have a list somewhere that I've just finished preparing.' He walked with effort to a writing desk in one corner of the room. It was closed, and when he opened the lid sheets of foolscap slid gracefully to the floor. Darroch rushed over to help. The sheets were full of scribbles from a shaky blue fountain pen: notes for a sermon or something similar. There were no paginations, so Darroch shuffled them into a random pile and placed them on top of the bureau. The old minister was still hunting in the desk for his list. He mumbled as he looked, peering closely at scraps of paper before dismissing them. He appeared to have forgotten that

Darroch was there, so the young minister, hands behind his back in a suitable pose, examined the glass bookcases which filled one complete wall of the room. The books were old, some with spines faded to obscurity. He saw many theological works, of course, but there were also books of Scottish and English literature and some historical works. He saw two big books concerning the history of central Fife.

'No, I can't find the blessed thing. What a nuisance.' The Reverend Walker closed the bureau sharply, catching many corners of foolscap in the edges of the desk as he did so. Darroch smiled. It was like a scene from an Ealing comedy. The old man peered at him. 'A cup of tea? No, something a little stronger I think, in order to celebrate your first parish proper. My goodness, how I remember my first parish, and that wasn't yesterday.' He shuffled over to a large cupboard and opened it, producing two crystal glasses from within. In another, smaller cupboard he finally found the whisky. Ice and water would not be necessary: he was of the traditional school. 'Nor the day before,' he said, chuckling as he filled the glasses, his hand shaking. He did not spill a drop. Darroch was still standing by the bookcases, hands behind back, face a blur to the old man. 'Come away and sit down,' he said. 'I can't see you over there. Sit here.'

Iain Darroch sat on the proffered settee. The Reverend Walker handed him a glass before slumping into an armchair, his breath heavy, his tongue glancing around his pale lips.

171

'Oh dear,' he said. He put his glass to his lips, paused, and toasted his visitor. 'Slàinte.'

'Your very good health, sir,' said Darroch, biting on the whisky before it could bite him.

There was a reflective silence. It was a good malt. The aroma of thick peat told Darroch that it came from the west coast, probably one of the Isles, rather than from the Highland glens. There was a good drop still left in his glass, and the old minister did not look particularly mean. Darroch took another sip.

'And how are you enjoying Carsden so far?' asked Reverend Walker. Darroch cleared his throat.

'Very much, sir. Yes, very much. The parishioners seem nice. A bit dour, perhaps, but I think that has a lot to do with economics.' Reverend Walker nodded.

'You are quite right. Economics. This used to be a thriving industrial town. Miners settled here from the Lothians and Lanarkshire when coal was discovered. Villages grew from nothing. The pit-owners built rows of houses which became miners' rows. These streets did not have names, only numbers. There was no room for imagination, you see. I believe some areas of Belfast still operate along the same lines. I was born in Thirteenth Street.' The old man spoke as a schoolmaster to an intelligent pupil. 'I've been coming back ever since, watching the village grow, then crumble. Watching decay set in like sugar on a tooth. It has not been pleasant, and the Church has been pretty powerless throughout. The best we've managed so far is to write a history of the parish. That was done by one of my predecessors at Cardell. I've a copy here somewhere. I must lend it to you. It tells how St Cuthbert settled here for a time and set up his church. It should interest you.'

'I'd like very much to read it, Reverend Walker.'

'Call me Alec. Most people do.'

'Very well. And I'm Iain.'

The old man nodded. 'Well, Iain,' he said, 'will you have another nip?'

Darroch reached his glass over towards his new friend.

'That's very interesting about St Cuthbert, Alec.'

'Indeed it is. But then Fife, including Carsden, is a very interesting region. I have several books on the subject. Really, it's quite a remarkable county. Were you born here?'

'Crail.'

'Oh, a glorious place, a really beautiful place. Of course, the East Neuk of Fife and central Fife are two different worlds. Industry has scooped the heart out of central Fife. We are living in an empty, echoing place. You may have noticed that?'

'I've noticed the looks in the eyes of some of my neighbours. In fact, one reason I wanted to see you was to ask you about one of them.'

'Ah yes,' the old man nodded, 'sadness. This was not a sad place, Iain, oh, maybe twenty years ago. But it does not take long to utterly destroy a sense of community. Oh dear, we're getting maudlin.'

Both men sipped their drinks and smacked their lips appreciatively.

'This is excellent whisky, Alec,' said Darroch, embarrassed by his own ingratiating tone. The Reverend Walker nodded.

173

'The water of life,' he said in all seriousness. 'The Church here, you know, is not what it was. I hope that you may be able to reverse the trend, but I quite doubt it, to be honest. The congregation of St Cuthbert's was once over three hundred when the population was considerably lower than it is now. My own church has suffered also. We both know that it is a general trend, but it is still appalling. I begin to wonder if this is truly a Godless age. If it is, then we are fools, are we not?'

Darroch reflected upon this. It was an old story, a story that came with the Ark. The Church was in decay, or at the very least relapse. Yet the coffers were full enough in some quarters. Churchmen never went hungry. They were satisfied with their lot. Perhaps there lay the root of the problem. What if ministers were paid by the number of people they converted per year? The churches would fill, or at least the ministry would try to perform its duties rather than sluggishly conforming to a lazy imitation of them. Darroch quite relished the thought of his reverie turning into reality. He was guilty of apathy himself, he realised. But now his host was speaking again.

'St Serf turned most of Fife into a Christian area. Prior to that Fifers had been picts, heathens. Much later, Fife was the home of the Seceders, a movement influenced by the teachings of Knox. There was much religious zeal and arguing in Fife at that time. More so than in any other county in Scotland. Coal-mining, it seems, went hand in hand with Christianity. The monks at Newbattle were Fife's first miners. And then Pope Pius the Second visited Scotland in the reign of Jamie the Saxt and was amazed to find beggars at the various churches receiving pieces of black stone as alms. This was coal, of course. According to records, Bowhill Colliery used to employ more men than any other Fife colliery. That was at the beginning of the 1900s, I believe. Bowhill Colliery used to lie towards Cardell. You've probably passed by it. It is still used for coal-washing, when there is not a strike on, but much of the original pit has been demolished. It was a big pit, and the population at that time must have been proud of it. They are still proud people, Iain, but they have lost anything to have a pride *in*. That's the crux of what's happening here. In some ways, however, I'm glad that we don't depend on mining as much as we used to. Goodness, how this last strike would have hit us. I can remember the first soup kitchens, back in the days of the General Strike. I was little more than a lad, but it was devastating, and it has left its indelible mark. There are modern soup kitchens now in places like Glenrothes and Cowden-beath. If we do not realise the full force of modern disputes, then it is because we were in many ways the forerunner of it. Children here run around in gangs and vandalise the shops and paint slogans on the walls. The adults beat each other up on Saturday night and drink too much and have bad marriages. It's a ghost town at nights because there are no amenities.' He sighed and shrugged his shoulders. 'There are social problems here that the Church cannot solve on its own. That's the truth. I apologise for my dejected tone, but it is better not to dream in a place like this.'

Darroch nodded thoughtfully. He sat with his hands folded in an imitation of prayer. 'Would you say then, Alec, that the people here are good in their hearts but have been let down by outside forces such as politics?'

The old man nodded, glass to his lips.

'Then,' continued Darroch, 'could you tell me about the attitude of these good people towards a woman called Mary Miller?'

The old man looked at him, and his gaze forced Darroch to lower his eyes into his own lap. There was a silence so powerful that for the first time Darroch could hear the grandfather clock ticking slowly in the hallway. The old minister sighed.

'That's a long and complex story, Iain. Should I tell it to you?'

'She is a member of my congregation, Alec.'

'Then shouldn't she be the one to tell you?'

'But would she tell me? Would you rather I got the story from some biased source?' Darroch had won the point. Alec Walker shrugged his crouched body and settled deep into his armchair.

'Very well,' he said, reaching for the bottle. 'Another refill is needed, I believe. I hope you are a good listener, Iain. This is not the most pleasant of stories.'

2

The dissolution was evident in and around Robbie's eyes. Sandy could hardly bear to look into those watery, red-rimmed pools. It was like gazing into a forbidden bedroom at the terminal patient within. He found a spot on Robbie's shirt collar where the material was fraying and concentrated his eyes there instead.

Robbie was wondering why Sandy had not been up to the mansion recently. The boy shrugged his shoulders and grunted. Robbie nodded his head but still looked at Sandy for an answer. Sandy shrugged again.

'The pressure of life,' he said finally.

'A fucking lot you would know about that, Alexander. A fucking lot.'

Sandy could not get things straight in his mind. This slouching youth was supposed to be evil, the ogre in the fairy story. The princess was being forced to slave for him. Yet Robbie still wore the guise of an innocent. He looked like his sister's keeper, yes, but not her pimp. Sandy was bursting to ask him outright about Rian's accusations. He blushed.

'What pressures of life have you got?' continued Robbie.

'Fuck off, Robbie. Stop talking about it.' This was man's talk; Rian was not present. Swearing was common speech among the men in the town. Some were known to communicate through swear-words alone. There were few words that Sandy did not know. He had been reading American crime novels for several years. Even serious literature in America used bad language. He was sure he knew words that no one else in Carsden knew. In the coming term, his last useless term at school, he was determined to use bad language in his essays for Andy Wallace. He was determined to register a protest about everything.

'You started it,' Robbie was saying.

'That's hardly fair.' Sandy managed to sound scoffing. Robbie shrugged his shoulders. He gazed at his companion, his eyes milky but keen.

'Not long now,' he said, to keep the conversation turning. In his life, Robbie talked to very few people, and fewer listened. He enjoyed Sandy's company more than he could say, and regarded him as a friend. He could not quite understand the change that had taken place in Sandy recently, but he knew that it had something to do with Rian. He knew that as well as he knew himself. Sandy seemed determined not to talk about it for the moment, but something in the boy's attitude told Robbie that he would talk about it soon enough, and that the conversation then would not be happy.

They walked quickly, but were held back by the steepness of The Brae. They were walking to Craigie Hill, just beyond Cardell, behind which a quarry was in operation. Craigie Hill was sheer at one side and sloping at the other. The tinkers' encampment was at the base of the sheer side. Sandy expected that one day a bulldozer would push the whole hillside down on top of the gypsies and their small modern caravans.

He had met Robbie near the school; a chance meeting. Previously, he had been wary of being seen with him, but the long summer had instilled a sense of carelessness in him, or rather recklessness, and so he walked with Robbie along the town's outskirts. Robbie was going to visit his Aunt Kitty. From her, Sandy hoped he would learn some truth.

Robbie coughed into his cupped hands, than spat noisily into the road.

'Do you feel it getting cooler these days?' he asked Sandy. The boy shook his head.

'Well,' said Sandy, 'the summer's not over yet. It's a long time since there was any rain. I can't say that I've noticed it cold. Are you feeling all right?'

'Fine, fine. Just a wee summer chill, that's all.' Sandy examined Robbie while he coughed again.

'Are you eating enough, Robbie?' he asked, embarrassed by the sympathy which was evident in his question.

'Oh aye, we eat well enough. We can't really eat hot food though, unless it's from the chip shop. My Aunt Kitty gives me a square meal whenever I visit. Rian's a decent enough cook, but there isn't the – what-do-you-call-thems? the facilities – in the mansion.'

'Aye.' Sandy nodded his head. He had never

known hunger or malnutrition. Hunger to him was the half-hour before lunch, soon appeased. Malnutrition was when his mother forgot the bacon for Sunday breakfast. He was like a fattened chick in a warm nest. Robbie, though, was a scavenger-hunter. He had to make kills if he was to eat, and had to make double the kills in order to feed his young sister. Was that the truth? Sandy could not see truth anywhere. He could see nothing but appearances. Things might or might not be what they seemed. He had written a poem about this problem, based upon a record by a rock group. He hoped to buy the group's new album with the money he would be given on his birthday. His sixteenth birthday was only two weeks away, a week after school restarted. Sixteen. Some things became legal. He could marry. That seemed absurd. He still could not go into pubs. He had promised himself that on his birthday he would go to Edinburgh by himself on the train. He would spend his money there. It would be an adventure. He had been there with his mother on childhood sightseeing trips, but this would be quite different. He would be sixteen. It seemed the perfect age. He did not think that he would like to be any older than sixteen, so long as he were still served in pubs.

Finally, at the top of the hill, they came to the encampment – four caravans and a couple of cars set on a patch of derelict ground in the shadow of the sheer rock face. Sandy knew the spot well. He could see it from the playing fields of his school. He knew that the locals had been trying to evict the gypsies ever since they had arrived there some ten months before. He did not know why they had not succeeded, but he knew that the bad feeling towards these people had shifted the balance of intolerance away from his mother, who might well be a witch in the eyes of the town but was still local born and bred and of decent parents. Sandy felt a pang of sadness. His mother's life had been one of peripheral contact, of balancing on a slender edge between acceptance and outright rejection, never knowing when the scales might perilously tip. It was horrible. She had no real friends. It was worse than having enemies. He felt his own resentment towards Andy Wallace lifting. It flew into the fine wind that curled around the field. It was scooped up over Craigie Hill itself and deposited in the growling quarry. The odds, Sandy knew, were against Andy Wallace as surely as they were against his mother. He prayed silently, to a God he was slowly recognising, that they might endure.

'That's my Aunt Kitty,' Robbie said. He was pointing a long arm towards a small, solid woman who emerged from one of the caravans and went behind it. Robbie shouted towards her, into the wind.

Her head appeared round the caravan. She waved, then the head disappeared again. She looked a bit like a rag-doll to Sandy. Her arm seemed a bag of stockings. When she came from behind the caravan, tugging at her patterned dress, Sandy saw that one sleeve of the dress was folded back and, presumably, tied behind her. The arm she had raised in welcome was her only arm. She chuckled now, displaying some black and crooked teeth. Her hair was tight with curlers and pins.

'You beast, Robbie, why haven't you been to see your old auntie before this? I was of a mind to come and see you meself.' There was no kissing, no handshakes. They stood a foot or two apart and smiled. Then she ushered them both towards the caravan. Sandy was having second thoughts. He recalled fairy stories his grandmother had told him. Her fairy stories could not be found in books. They came from her head, as if it were some great repository of knowledge. Sandy had the feeling that, because she told her stories with her eyes closed and without the aid of books, his grandmother's tales had been real. This had shocked him into full attentiveness as a listener, and he had forgotten few of them. He remembered one now. It concerned a young girl who was taken to a gypsy camp and made to dance until she died, but when she died her spirit had been strong and she was able to cure her little sister who had been crippled. Sandy knew that in essence the story was concerned with not fearing death, but there was something more to it. Who could say that he was not walking into a sacrifice? Rian had told him never to trust Robbie. Now he was in the hands of both Robbie and the aunt who, according to Rian, had wanted to use her cruelly. He had been stupid to come to this place.

A large mongrel dog, as if confirming his growing fears, barked at him viciously. It was tethered to one of the caravans, but only by a rope. He backed away from it, and in so doing edged closer to the old, cackling woman and her caravan. Robbie approached the animal and stroked it. It ignored him and went on barking and baring its teeth at Sandy.

'Come on and make friends,' Robbie called to him, patting the snarling beast.

'Come inside, dear,' coaxed the old woman with her dark mouth.

Sandy tore himself in two. Part of him ran to safety, but that was his spirit self; his body climbed the two iron steps slowly and was inside the caravan.

The woman stooped low over her cooker and ignited the gas. She pushed a blackened kettle on to the ring. Sandy inspected the cramped interior. There was nothing romantic or sensational about it. A small television sat on the only table, wired to a car battery on the floor. There were two bench-seats facing into this table, the whole contrivance becoming a small double bed when adjusted. Sandy liked caravans. He liked their clever compactness, not an inch of space wasted. He realised that life in the town was a little like that. He looked at the paintings on the walls, crude, cheap reproductions in plastic frames. There was no toilet. He remembered the woman emerging from behind the caravan. He could taste mothballs at the back of his throat.

'Cup of tea, son?'

'Please.' The old woman grinned at him again.

'Scared of me, son? People are. People say it's because of me teeth. They say I should get new ones, but the price of these things is ridiculous. Besides, these have done me well enough over the years. I can still chew me meat with them, so there you are.'

So there he was. 'Yes,' he managed to reply.

'You a friend of our Robbie's? Robbie's not got many friends, has he?' She was watching the kettle as it began to steam. She moved to the tiny sink next to the stove and rinsed three cups in a thin trickle of water from the faucet. 'Bit of a loner like. Gypsies have to be, haven't they, son? Not much else open to them. Still, I wish the townies – no offence to yourself, son – would stop bothering us.' She glared at him for a moment, so that the point was not lost on him. 'It's a respectable life that we lead. Ancient, too. Goes back before towns was even invented. You look it up in your library, son. Gypsies has been here since the country itself.' She chuckled. It was, Sandy realised, a matronly sound rather than a wicked one. He could talk.

'My mother's supposed to be a witch,' he said. He wondered why he had said that. Perhaps, he thought, to show that he understood.

'Is she now? Oh yes, I seem to remember being told about the town's witch. Ah yes. Cause of bad luck, wasn't she?'

'She's not really a witch.'

'Gracious me, of course she's not. Witches never existed, except in people's minds. All there was in the olden days was women and some men who believed in herbal cures and in folklore and in the wish to fly. Witches? We're all witches in one way or another. Witches was the invention of mankind, son. We're all witches beneath the skin.' Her words sounded wise to Sandy. She poured boiling water into a battered teapot. He wanted suddenly to be her friend.

'My name's Sandy,' he said. She smiled and nodded. His eyes were mesmerised by the loose fold of material pinned behind her with a large safety pin.

'You're wondering about me arm, Sandy,' she said, her back still towards him. He was stunned. It was as if she had really read his mind. He remained silent and she turned towards him and chuckled again. 'Course you are.' Then she went to the open door. Sandy noticed that it was growing dark outside, though it was only two o'clock. Clouds were gathering for a storm. The drought was about to break. 'Robbie!' shouted the old woman, 'Tea's up!' The dog barked keenly as Robbie sprinted to the caravan. There were specks of water on his shoulders as he entered, stooping.

'That's the rain on,' he said. 'Looks like a heavy one, though.'

Sandy began, almost instantly, to hear the raindrops on the roof, like sharp raps against a drum. Carsden had a fine pipe band, but they would have been hard-pressed to play the tune that was soon dancing on the caravan's skin-tight roof. They sipped the tea around the small table, Sandy's knees rubbing uncomfortably against those of the woman. They listened to the rain as if it were music.

'That's summer over,' said Kitty. She winked at the boy. There was a trace of matter in one of her eyes. Sandy wondered if the eye, like her arm, was useless.

'You could be right, Kitty,' said Robbie. 'I was telling Sandy that I've noticed a cold air this past few days.'

'A cold air?' Kitty stared hard at her nephew. 'Cold air nothing. Look at you. You've been drinking too much and not eating a thing. You're dying of the wrong diet, Robbie. *She's* to blame. You should come back here where you belong.'

'What about Rian? She belongs here too.' Robbie, having said this, supped his tea and kept his eyes on the table. There was a silence, broken only by the heavy battering of the rain upon the roof.

'Leave her to her ruin,' said Kitty, her mouth brushing the edge of her chipped cup.

'I can't do that, Kitty.'

There was a pause, the most excruciating silence Sandy had ever heard. The air seemed tense with thunder. The rain was easing.

'Don't I bloody know it!' exploded the old woman. She glanced at Sandy and calmed down. 'Sorry, son. You shouldn't have to listen to this. It's the same every time Robbie comes back.' She chuckled hollowly. 'Will I make you something to eat?' She rose from the table. Sandy looked at Robbie, who was staring out of the rain-daubed window.

'Any smokes, Kitty?'

She rummaged in the pocket of her dress and threw a small pack of tobacco, a thin roll of papers and a box of matches on to the table.

'Ta,' said Robbie. The threat of thunder eased,

Sandy remembered that rain comes after thunder, not before it. He was sweating. The air was still and thick. The rain would freshen everything. It was great to walk about after rain. He hoped he could escape soon.

'Sandy here fancies Rian,' said Robbie casually as he rolled a cigarette. Sandy was startled by his friend's cruelty.

'Is that surprising?' muttered Kitty. She turned towards them. 'Remember what I said about witches, Sandy? I take it all back. Witches do exist, and that bitch is one of them. Steer clear of her. That's my advice and always has been.'

'Full of the milk of human kindness, that's my Aunt Kitty.' Robbie lit his cigarette and winked at Sandy. Kitty shuffled over from the stove. Her hand snaked out viciously and she slapped Robbie so hard that the cigarette flew out of his mouth and into Sandy's lap. Sandy picked it up quickly and held it. There was a long, staring silence before the woman shuffled back to her stove. Robbie held out his hand for the cigarette. He puffed on it until it seemed to ignite from nothing.

'That girl is nothing but trouble and you know it.'

Sandy wondered if this were an act for his benefit. It did not seem like one. So was Rian lying to him then? Was she more than she seemed? Who could he trust to tell him the truth? The answer was simple – no one.

The sun broke through the fine sheen of rain. Sandy stared at the small window. Dirt was now visible on the inside of the glass. The faint smell of soup touched his nostrils and pushed further back the tang of mothballs. It was a good smell; rich like the soup his grandmother had made, vegetables thick with a hint of stock. His stomach felt suddenly empty, though he had eaten not two hours before. The pot was soon steaming. Two plates were placed on the table, either side of the small television, then two slices of thin white bread, and two discoloured spoons. Sandy warily examined the spoon before him. He knew that it would taste of metal and the thought made him shiver.

'Put out that roll-up while you eat.' It was a soft command. Robbie flicked the butt out of the window.

'Satisfied?' he said. Kitty ignored him. She served the soup and squeezed in beside Sandy again. He felt his leg tingle as hers touched it. He drew it away awkwardly, and felt his other leg brushing against Robbie.

'Are you still at school, Sandy?' asked Kitty.

'Just until Christmas.' He drank the soup without letting the spoon enter his mouth. Kitty was studying him.

'And you've sat your exams then?'

He nodded. 'I got the results this morning.'

'You never told me that,' said Robbie, taking big gulps of soup.

'You never asked.'

'Were the results good?' asked Kitty. Sandy nodded. 'Your mum must be pleased, eh?'

'She doesn't know yet. I'm going to tell her tonight. It'll be a surprise for her.'

Kitty chuckled again. She was rolling a cigarette of her own. She did the whole thing expertly with her one hand and her teeth. Really, it was hard to believe that she had only one arm. Sandy tried not to stare.

'You know how this happened?' she said, the cigarette wagging in her mouth. 'I'll tell you. I was mauled by a dog that was set on me by a farmer up north. Near Inverness, wasn't it, Robbie? He saw me coming up his drive and he set his bloody dog on me, the bastard. I wouldn't see no doctor afterwards, you see. Then it hurt too much, but by then it was too late. They had to amputate it. Robbie was about thirteen then, wasn't you?' He nodded, his eyes on the empty bowl in front of him. 'Aye, thirteen he was. You know what we did? A few of the menfolk and wee Robbie here, they snaked up to the farm one afternoon while the farmer was about his business and they killed the dog.' She chuckled mirthlessly. Her eyes were strong upon Sandy's. His stomach turned the soup in a slow, sickening revolution. The matter in her left eye was like a tiny maggot, alive and wriggling. 'They stoned it to death and threw it into the farmhouse. We had to get out of that neck of the country in a hurry, I can tell you. But it was worth it.' She laughed this time. Her mouth was a deep red cavern surrounded by teeth like chippings of coal. Robbie was scraping his spoon across the base of his bowl.

'I've got to go now,' said Sandy. 'Excuse me. Thank you for the soup and the tea.' He was aware of his false formality, aware that it showed his weakness. He blanched. The old woman slid from her seat to let him out.

'I'll stay on for a bit,' said Robbie. 'Aunt Kitty and me have things to talk about.' He reached across the table for another roll-up.

'It was nice seeing you,' Sandy said to Kitty.

'And you, son.' She chuckled, knowing the truth. 'Come and see us any time.'

He stepped outside and breathed in the grass-heavy air. The dog stood up and barked again. He ignored it. A man watched him from the door of one of the other caravans. He was scratching his grizzled chin as if sizing the boy up for a potential meal. Sandy, his heart thudding, walked smartly away.

'Sandy!'

He turned and saw Robbie running awkwardly towards him, as if he had never run in his life. Sandy waited for him. Robbie walked the last few yards and puffed on his cigarette. He stopped beside his friend and stared into the distance. He mumbled something, then looked back towards the caravans.

'Promise you won't tell Aunt Kitty,' he repeated. 'Promise you won't ever tell her or anyone else.' Sandy nodded. 'Promise,' said Robbie.

'I promise.'

'Okay.' He took a gulp of air. His eyes were like a mongrel's. 'Listen then. We never killed the dog. None of us had the guts. We sat in the woods for a while, had a smoke, then went back to the camp and told everyone our story. We said that we'd best be moving. We moved away so that she wouldn't find out that we'd not done it. It would have killed her

190

and killed us if we'd confessed. So don't feel bad about it, okay?' He put a hand gently on Sandy's shoulder. Sandy nodded. He was about to say something, but Robbie was already starting away. 'See you later,' he called back. 'Come up to the house.'

'Fine,' yelled Sandy. He walked away, sure in his heart that Rian had been lying to him about her brother and her aunt. He did not want to believe it, yet the evidence was before his eyes like the scenery. He could accept it or not; it was reality. He frowned. There was something he had meant to ask Aunt Kitty. The meaning of an itchy nose. That was it: what was the meaning of an itchy nose?

3

George Patterson had locked the door, pulled down the blind, and was busying himself with the small change at his till when a sharp rapping on the door told him that his friend was waiting to be let in. He came from behind the counter, crossed to the door, peered through the glass, and, a smile settling on his face, drew back the lock.

'Hello, George. Busy day?'

'Not bad, Matt. Yourself?'

Matt Duncan scratched his cheek. He had not shaved that day and the bristles were iron-grey and hard.

'Doing away, George,' he said. 'That's all we can do, eh? Just doing away.'

'Aye, Matt, it's the truth.' Patterson relocked the door and ushered the smaller man through to the back room where hair was occasionally cut. 'Go on through, Matt,' he said. 'You know your way. I'll be with you in a minute.' He went back to his counting, his fingers springy and agile. He totalled the day, scratched with his pen on a piece of paper, put the paper and the notes in his pocket, closed the till and locked it. Then he walked slowly through to the back room, opened another door, and was in a tiny room which was comfortably furnished. Matt Duncan was opening a can of beer.

'It's grand to have a beer these nights,' he said, handing the can to Patterson.

George Patterson sat down. He knew that Matt Duncan was a bit of a rogue, but he was an old friend. Patterson did not have many friends. He rejected invitations the way other men refused to play with their children. Yet he had known Matt Duncan, who was five years older than him, since his schooldays. Only in the past five or so years, however, had they become good friends. Both had bitter pasts to complain about, and both had patient ears as long as they knew that their own complaints would be listened to eventually. Patterson watched the foxy old man sink into an ancient armchair. The room contained two armchairs, a small writing desk, and a fridge. The beer had been kept in the fridge. It was chilled, and the bubbles caused Patterson to burp silently and often. It was gassy stuff this; not the same as you got in the pub. Eventually they would go out to the pub, but it was nice to sit and talk together first.

'Weather turned stormy today,' said Matt Duncan.

'Aye,' said Patterson, 'but not before time. It's been a good few weeks since we had some rain. I could see the paper bags and rubbish blowing about outside, just like tumbleweeds in a Western.'

They both chuckled, sharing as they did a liking for old cowboy films. Duncan liked novels about the West, too, but George Patterson found them banal. They did not discuss these novels in case they should argue. Neither could afford to lose the other, though neither really knew why.

'It was terrible. I got caught in the rain as I was going down to the bookie's.'

'Win anything today, Matt?'

Duncan's face screwed in disgust. 'Not a bloody thing,' he said. 'But Dod Mathieson, a man that's not needing money, he won naturally.' His voice was bitter. He hated the man who had won. 'I'd like to know how he manages to win so bloody much and I lose. I think he's in on some game with the manager of that shop. They're always gassing together, yet the bugger would hardly give me the time of day. Aye, there's something funny there all right. You take my word for it.'

Patterson shook his head in sympathy. Yes, the world seemed cruel to Matt Duncan. The grass was always greener. You lose a son, you lose your job. You've lost everything, and you're bitter. Patterson was not himself a bitter man, not really. He fed on guilt instead. He was, he knew, worse off than Matt Duncan, for he could not reveal his guilt, though often he had come close. Poor Hugh. What good had it all been? He had to feed perpetually on his shame, with no one knowing. Well, hardly anyone.

'Mind you, Matt Duncan's not a man to go telling on people. If they've got shady dealings, it's up to the shop-owner to find out. He must be raking it in if he can afford to ignore a swindle like the nice one they've got going.' The conspiracy was now an incontrovertible fact for Duncan. He drank his beer noisily, as if its flavour were the taste of his rage.

'Are you sure there *is* a swindle, Matt?' ventured Patterson hesitantly. 'Couldn't it all be luck?'

'Of course I'm sure, George,' snapped back the small, sharp-faced man. 'What do you take me for? I ken what their game is. You can't keep anything like that hidden from Matt Duncan. I'm too fly for them, you see. They think I'm dunnert.' His mouth was a savage twist and his breath came short and noisily. Patterson kept quiet and drank his lager while the tumult continued. There were a lot of twisted men like Matt Duncan throughout the mining towns of Fife. Usually they were not the best workers, had lived bitter, ignorant married lives, and had been brought up in similar households. In other words, their hate was handed down to them from their parents, handed down through the generations like a christening shawl. It seemed an attitude peculiar to the working class. Patterson often mused over it. It appeared to him an easy way out, an excuse for not having done anything in life. If you succeeded you were 'lucky', or a crook; other factors did not enter into it. If you failed, you had never had a chance. Everything had been against you in the first place. A shiver went through Patterson. He had been living in this community for fifty-five years. Luckily, his father had been a professional person. That was regarded as his lucky beginning. Only once had he felt as Duncan felt all the time. Just that once. His mind recoiled from the self-hatred and the grotesque thought of that isolated time. He shook his can.

'Empty?' asked Duncan.

'Yes, Matt. Very empty,' said Patterson thought-fully. 'I'll get my coat and we can go to the hotel for a proper drink.'

'Fine,' said Duncan, patting his pockets. 'Ach,' he said as always, 'I've forgotten my wallet again, George, and that thief of a bookmaker cleaned me out. Shall I run up to the house and fetch it?' Patterson, as always, shook his head.

'No need for that, Matt. No need for that at all.' He even smiled.

His mother had invited Andy Wallace round for an evening meal. They were planning to go to Kirkcaldy afterwards to see a film. The three of them sat around the seldom-used dining table and the only sound for a time was that of good cutlery against china.

'Haven't you had your results yet, Sandy?' said Andy Wallace finally.

'Got them this morning,' replied Sandy, toying with a potato. His mother put down her fork. Her hands lay against either side of her plate as if she were about to ask for more.

'Well?' she said.

'Five As, a B, and a C.'

'Well, well, well.' Andy Wallace sat back in his chair, smiling, looking across at Mary. 'That's a very good performance. Better than your marks in your prelims.'

Mary Miller tried to squeeze her son's hand, but he slid it away from her and scratched his nose.

'With results like those,' continued Andy Wallace,

'you'd be daft to leave at Christmas. Why not stay on for your Highers?'

'Yes, Sandy. Stay on.'

Sandy looked at his mother and his English teacher. He was surprised by the emotion in his mother's voice. Andy Wallace, though trying not to show it, was astonished at himself. A little while ago he had been hoping that Sandy would leave school at the earliest opportunity. Now here he was telling the boy to stay on. He was pleased at his morality; he had the teaching reflex.

'I'll think about it,' said Sandy.

'You do that,' said Andy Wallace. Mary smiled at both of them. It was like being part of a family. Recently she had been worrying about Andy's attitude towards her. For how long would he continue to be so patient? She could not know, but she sensed his growing frustration. If only she could make love, just the once, then it would be all right. If only.

'You could go to university with marks like that if you were to stick in,' said Andy, anxious not to let the table recede into another silence. He pronged four peas on to the end of his fork and grabbed them between his teeth. 'They're as good as I ever got,' he said.

Sandy, however, had retreated back into his meal. He cut the meat delicately. He concentrated on his plate. He did not want this conversation to continue. His mother's cheeks were a proud red. She looked more than ever like a princess trapped in a tower. Sandy remembered the poem he had written about

Rian. It could have applied just as well to his mother. Her hair was tied simply behind her. Silver through black. Metal through water. She seemed to glimmer in the pale light. Sandy was looking forward to having the house to himself for the evening. He was going to invite Rian round to visit in his mother's absence. He smiled at the thought. His mother noticed his smile and returned it. He had not the heart to turn away from her in her happiness.

It was quiet at the mansion. A cold breeze ruffled the ancient oaks and carried the cries of the golfers towards him from the first tee. He waited until they had moved off across the fairway before he climbed the pipe. He was an adventurer now. Nothing stood in his way. He only hoped Robbie was still at the caravan. It seemed a forlorn hope, but he would get Rian away despite any move made by her brother. He had to take her to neutral territory (or, if the bravado held up, to *his* home territory) in order to put certain questions to her.

He kicked in the shoddy piece of board, hoisted his legs over the sill, and was in. He walked quickly through the shadowy corridor, looking neither left nor right, and opened the door to her room. There was nobody there. He walked inside anyway, not believing his bad fortune.

'Oh, it's you.'

His heart missed a beat in fright. He turned. She had been hiding behind the door.

'I heard the window,' she said. 'It didn't sound like Robbie, so I hid.' She was facing him now, close. He

198

took a step towards her and their lips met, their tongues twisting like tiny serpents at the mouth of a cave. He held her waist. Her hair touched the backs of his hands. When he opened his eyes this time he saw that hers were ecstatically closed. The black slits of her lashes gave more passion to his kiss. She pulled away.

'We're going out. Okay?' Sandy's voice, prepared to be manly, was trembling and uncertain.

'Where?' Her eyes were wide. She folded her long arms around herself. She was cold. Sandy remembered that her skin had been deathly to the touch.

'Somewhere warm,' he said. 'I thought you might like to see where I live. My mum's out with her boyfriend. They won't be back till midnight. Would you like to?' Now he was the pleading schoolboy with a would-be friend. His eyes were as wide as he could make them. Rian messed with her hair.

'I should wait for Robbie. He's been gone all day.'

'He's at his Aunt Kitty's.'

'Is he?' She was genuinely surprised. 'That's not where he said he was going. How do you know?' As she moved to the window he noticed that her face was puffy from sleep, as innocent as a new-born. She leaned against the half-boarded window.

'I went with him this afternoon for a little while.' Her eyes darted to him like stinging things.

'You did?' she asked, her voice quivering.

'Yes, to find out the meaning of an itchy nose. You remember.'

'Oh, but that was a long time ago.' She was hesitant. Then she smiled. 'Well, if my brother can go off to our scheming aunt's without telling me, I can go with my friend to his house. Isn't that right?' She approached him and took his arm. 'Shall we go?' she said. He smiled, took off his jacket, and made her put it on.

'Oh, Sandy.' Her face was suddenly ill again, only half alive. 'I'm scared of what they might be planning there. You know they hate me. Everybody there hates me. They want to use me and hurt me and . . .' She broke off to cry, her head bowed to his shoulder. 'Oh, Sandy,' she said again. He lifted her head, kissed her brow perfunctorily, and began to manoeuvre her towards the corridor. He placed one arm around her. Her feet slid across the floorboards as if she were learning to walk again after an accident. Sandy's groin pulsed. He could not believe it. He was not even sixteen yet. Soon he might join Colin in knowledge. Soon he might have something to tell the gang. He felt strong.

They crossed several fences and trudged through several fields to reach the back of his house unseen. In Carsden, secrecy was well-nigh impossible, but Sandy felt that they had done a good job. Though Rian complained, he did not tell her the reason for his furtive actions.

In the garden, they scraped mud from their shoes on to the edge of the path. The garden needed digging, and he promised himself silently that he would put some work into it at the weekend. He opened the door to the kitchen, with his own key which had been made a long time ago without his mother's knowledge, and, when the door was open, made an extravagant gesture towards Rian. She bowed gracefully and entered. He closed the door behind them.

Now that Rian was in his home, Sandy felt confused. Her aroma was everywhere. It made the house different, made it strange to him. He showed her around like a trainee estate agent. In his room, the last to be investigated, he sat casually on his bed and asked her to sit down. She sat beside him, her hands stretched along her lap. He pecked her cheek. She smiled, but looked apprehensive. She was examining the posters on his walls and his two rows of books.

'You've got a lot of books,' she said.

His bravado faded like a song that had gone on for too long. He suggested that they go back downstairs for a drink and she readily agreed. As they left the room, Sandy patted his bedspread flat again, erasing the mark of her from it for ever. He was flushed and had assumed a nervous cough.

In the living room they watched television and drank a little whisky, not enough to be visibly missing from the bottle. Rian was entranced by the television screen. She sat close to it, her face turning the rainbow colours of the programmes as she flicked from channel to channel. She stroked the carpet with her free hand as if it were a slumbering cat. Outside it was raining again. They would get soaked going back through the fields. Sandy had closed the curtains. He had turned off the lights. The television was their magic lantern. He put on a small electric fire and Rian shifted close to it. She had her thumb in her mouth now that she had settled on one channel to watch. Sandy sat on the floor beside her, his feelings for the slender girl jumbled but passionate.

'Rian,' he said, but she did not answer. 'Rian.' This time she grunted, glanced at him, smiled, pecked his cheek, and turned back to the television. He reached behind his back towards the wall and silently dislodged the plug of the television. The picture fizzled and faded from the screen. Only the red of the fire illuminated them in the sudden silence.

'What's wrong with it, Sandy?' Her voice was childlike. 'Have you done something? You have, haven't you?'

He looked aghast. 'Me? I've not done anything.' He pushed a few of the buttons on the television, felt behind the set, frowned, and finally said, 'It must be the fuse.' He brought a screwdriver from one of the drawers and, pulling the plug completely out of the socket, began to open the casing. 'Listen,' he said. 'Can we talk about things?' He said this as he made his thorough inspection of the plug's interior. Rian looked on like a spectator at an operation.

'What things?' she said slowly, her curiosity shifting.

'That day down at Kirkcaldy. What you told me. What you said about Robbie. Was that all true? Or were you making it up?' His eyes were still firmly on the plug. He spoke as if preoccupied. She looked on, never glancing at him.

'Of course it's true,' she said. 'Why do you say that?'

He shrugged. 'Just a feeling, that's all. To tell you the truth,' now he did look at her, 'I don't think Robbie would do that, what you said. That's why I'm wondering.' He bent to his work. The screwdriver forced the fuse out from the casing. 'Ah ha,' he said. Her face was crimson beside his, her cheeks hot from the fire. She edged closer.

'Sandy,' she said, 'every word was true. I swear to God.' She made a crude attempt at crossing herself. 'Every word. Robbie is horrible. You can't see that, but he is. He doesn't let you see him as he really is.' Her words became choked. Tears sharpened in her eyes. As on the sea-wall that day, she did not allow them to fall. She looked at him. 'Robbie tells men about me. He gets them to give him money, then I have to toss them. You know what that is, don't you?' He blushed, nodded, continued to examine the fuse. Inside he was a single pulse. 'Or else he tells me to go and find men for myself, then I've to give him the money. He hits me if I don't get any money. Sometimes I steal so that I don't have to do it, but that just makes him think that I'm good at it. Oh, Sandy.' Although his head was bowed, she could see that he was crying. He wept silently, but his shoulders jerked in spasms. She put her arm around him. He did not know why he was crying – it could even have been jealousy. He had not cried for a long time, perhaps not since his grandmother had died. He hardly knew the meaning of the thing. Rian saw in his tears, in the traces streaked down both

203

cheeks, his humanity. Her own were small things by comparison. 'Oh, Sandy,' she said. 'Why are you crying?'

She might as well have been asking him for his definition of love. He shook his head and sniffed. His nose was running like a baby's. He felt his cheeks flush in embarrassment. So much for bravado. So much for the great lover. He was still a fucking virgin baby at heart. He blew his nose angrily. Her hands were on his face. He put his arms around her and slowly pulled her to the floor. They lay still together. Sandy stared at the ceiling while Rian stroked his face and his neck. When she made to sit up he pulled her towards him again and kissed her as forcefully as he could. If he was her boyfriend, then didn't he deserve it? He drew her in towards him like a twin just before birth. She resisted a little. He rolled over on top of her and, after a moment's significant eye contact, placed his hand on her tiny breast. She closed her eyes. He moved his hand downwards, watching her face. His hand was as sensitive as the nerve in a tooth. He discovered every ripple in the material of her skirt. His fingers touched her knee. He began to slide his hand upwards again. Her eyes opened like sentries caught napping. She pushed him, rolled away from him, and stood up. She was nearly shouting, her voice a tremor.

'No, Sandy, not with you, Sandy! I won't. I won't.' She paused, breathing heavily. 'You have no right.' She looked away. 'I don't mean it like that.'

'I've got some money upstairs if that's what you

mean.' He thought that a worthy line, like something a film actor would have said. She glared at him
and started to walk towards him. He knew, as surely
as Robbie had known in the caravan, what was
coming. He reeled from her blow. She looked strong
now, and vicious. She spat words at him.

'You can't talk like that. I won't let you. You're
just like the rest. You're like all of them. I hate you.'
She turned, looking for her coat. She had no coat,
only his jacket. She walked to the door. He chased
after her.

'Don't go,' he said. She stood at the kitchen door,
her back to him. 'I apologise. I didn't know what I
was doing. Please wait. I've got a present for you.
Will you wait?' She nodded, her long hair waving.
'Okay,' he said.

He ran up the stairs three at a time, his speciality,
and went into the cold back bedroom. Had it ever
been a bedroom? Yes, for a short time before his
grandmother had died he had slept in it. Perhaps for
two years. He could not remember. Probably his
mother had slept in it too, when Uncle Tom had
been too big to share with her. But it was a cold
room. He remembered having nightmares in it. He
pushed open the trunk and selected one of the many
woollen articles from it. It was a beautiful shawl, one
of his grandmother's creations. He closed the lid and
hurried downstairs. She had not moved, apparently.

'Here,' he said. Still she would not turn. He placed
the shawl gently around her shoulders. 'A present,'
he said. She seemed to examine its corners. Then she
turned. She was smiling. They embraced. Her hair

was clean like a wet sea-shore. He stroked it. They stood like that for a while.

'Listen,' he said, 'I think I've got an idea.' He spoke in her ear, his face towards the kitchen. 'Would you like to come and live here with us? I could talk to my mum. She would understand. I'm sure she would. She's sort of an outsider too, remember.'

'Oh, I'd like that I think, Sandy. But I can't leave Robbie. He'd, well, I don't know what he'd do without me. But . . .' Her voice tailed off. He could feel that she was torn between something like familial masochism and freedom.

'But listen,' he said excitedly. 'I'd make sure Robbie was all right.'

'How?' Her voice warmed to him.

'What about if I gave him money, enough to see him through for a while?'

'Money?'

'Like buying you from him, but really buying you your freedom.' His voice was heated. He felt like an old philanthropist. He was acting out a history lesson.

'Money,' she whispered.

'Yes.' He hardly heard her. 'I'd give him some money.'

'How much?' He smiled at her swift words. He hugged her to him and his eyes gazed like new stars through the door of the kitchen, through the back door, right out into space itself. Anything was possible. Anything.

'Oh, I don't know.'

'Maybe thirty or forty pounds?' she said.

'Forty?' His voice was unconcerned.

'But fifty would be better, wouldn't it? He'd take fifty.'

'Fifty?' It seemed like a great deal of money, but it had to be a bargain.

'But where would you get fifty pounds, Sandy?' Where indeed. Schemes loomed in his mind. Anything was possible, but what was probable?

'I'd get it,' he said, feeling heroic. She pulled away from him a little, saw confidence in his face, gasped, and kissed him three times quickly.

'Oh, I love you, Sandy. I really think I do.' She stroked her shawl. 'And thanks for my present. It's lovely. I've never been given a present before, honest. I really think I love you.' She kissed him again. He was chuckling now. He shrugged his shoulders.

'It's an old shawl,' he said. 'No use here. We've got plenty. It'll keep you warm at night. We don't want you getting cold.' He looked at his watch. 'My God, it's past eleven! Come on, I'll see you back to the mansion. You look like a lady in that thing.' He nodded at the shawl as she pulled it around herself. 'You really do.'

He switched off the lights pensively, hoping he would have enough time left on his return to clean up before his mother came back with Andy Wallace. Fifty pounds. It was the price of a stereo. The price of ten records. He would get it, but he could not think of a likely source at the moment. That was for the future anyway. For the moment he was happy to be climbing the fence behind his girlfriend, remembering her climbing the drainpipe, leaping into mud and grass, walking heavily through the boggy fields and the drizzle to her castle.

4

The air was chilled in the manse. Iain Darroch rubbed his hands together as he entered, letting the books under his arm slip noisily to the floor. He ignored them for the moment, switched on the fire in his adequate sitting room, then returned to the hallway, closed the door properly, picked up the books and, his coat still wrapped around him, returned to the faint but growing glow of the fire.

September. The leaves were turning. The summer was over. He looked towards the long winter ahead with morose eyes. In winter the sap really was at its lowest ebb, spiritually as well as physically. He did not relish the prospect. He made some tea in the clutterless kitchen and brought it through to the fireside. He sat down on the sheepskin rug. Sipping the tea, he pulled a book towards him from the small coffee table.

The conversation with Reverend Walker had fired something in him, some need to know his parish as one would know one's ancestors. He had read several books from Reverend Walker's collection, and had now brought three more from Kirkcaldy Public Library. Carsden had a strange, fascinating past. Fife itself was notable as a historic county, but it was Carsden that really interested him. He began reading. His notebook lay beside him, a fountain pen hooked over its edge. Fife, he had found, was riddled with superstition. The Church had never been as strong, perhaps, as was thought. Witches had been burned in Fife right up until the end of the seventeenth century, and those figures came from incomplete records. Who could say what might have happened thereafter? Robert Baillie, a Presbyterian minister of the time, had recorded that in 1643 thirty witches had been burned in Fife in a few months. James Hogg had written or procured a lyric ballad called 'The Witch of Fife', and there was also a well-known poem called 'The Witch of Pittenweem'. Pittenweem was near to Darroch's birthplace, and the whole East Neuk appeared to be riddled with tales of witchcraft. Darroch found it all fascinating.

The facts had piled up in his notebook randomly at first, but then more selectively. He thought he had found a kind of connection between two aspects of Fife's history. Cromwell had selected Burntisland as one of the first places to attack (*circa* 1651?) because of its importance as a port. An Act of 1842 prohibited women from working underground. Thereafter sprang up the superstition that it was unlucky for a woman to venture into a pit. Pit. The very word stirred him. A pit had been opened by the Queen at Glenrothes in the late 1950s (?). She inspected it. A few years later it was forced to close due to flooding. It was seen as part of the superstitious truth. The Earl of Wemyss had owned many of the Fife collieries, though not those around Carsden. Some of these pits were sunk, according to family records, on the sites of what had been witch-burning places. The people had been given chunks of coal as alms. Coal was a magic rock, a black diamond, mysterious and life-giving.

Carsden had its own witch-burning site, not a colliery now but the local park, which meandered down to a shallow river, aptly named the Ore. Suspected (proven?) witches were placed in a barrel by the good people of the village, and the barrel was then coated with tar and ignited. A lid was nailed on, and the whole contraption was rolled down the meandering slope where children now played and into the river. The screams carried downriver, the barrel smouldering and fizzing like a firework. It was horrible, and it was happening in the seventeenth century. Three hundred years ago. Mary Miller was, in a sense, lucky.

The random jottings had begun to connect for Darroch. Mining, it seemed to him, was a superstitious occupation, and it had gone hand in hand with the superstitions and witch-burnings of that age. He thought of Mary Miller. Poor woman. The superstitions held fast, gripped by the downtrodden class as a means of creating scapegoats for their bad fortune. It was the easy solution. Instead of raging at the landowners or looking to themselves, they merely picked on an outsider and branded her a witch, blaming her for any misfortune, any hiccup of economics. That made the villagers feel better in their hungry bitterness. They fed on it like a fire feeds on coal. Darroch checked himself. These were his parishioners. He should have patience with them, and Christian tolerance. It was hard, though, with all their chiselling ways. He read his book again, the fire warming his clothes so that they smelled newly laundered and ironed.

The very name of the town worried him. Carsden. It was named, presumably, after Carsden Woods just outside the town. The den was a valley near these woods. But what about the etymology of Carsden itself? There were two possibilities, one of which seemed ominous. He had travelled to Edinburgh, to the National Library, for these notes. He had looked at Grant's *Scottish National Dictionary*, Craigie's *A Dictionary of the Older Scottish Tongue*, Chambers' *Scots Dictionary*, and *Jamieson's Scottish Dictionary*. He had found a kind of consensus. 'Car' meant left or left-handed. It also meant (presumably because left-handedness was considered ominous by superstitious people) sinister, fatal, or wrong in a moral sense. 'Carlin' (also 'carling', 'carline', 'karlyn', 'karling') meant a witch. This was especially true when used in the Lothians, Ayrshire (another notorious witch-hunting area) and Fife. This had led Darroch to deduce that Carsden would mean den of the witch. He researched into other similar place-names. Carlops, on the road south from Edinburgh to Biggar, was named after its imposing rock. He found that there were two versions of the etymology. One stated that it was a place from where witches had flown, originally Carlings-Loups. The other claimed that the rock was the site from where villagers would hurl suspected witches, shouting at them to fly now if they could. If Carlops derived its name from witches, then why not Carsden? In *Jamieson's Dictionary*, however, he found that 'car', used as the initial syllable of a place-name, could mean 'fortified place', which would mean that Carsden had been a fortified den. No history of the area, however, spoke of fortifications until the time of St Cuthbert and the building of the kirk. It was a puzzle. Wickedly, he preferred to think of the former as the truth.

But no, no 'witches' had ever flown away to safety from Carlops Hill. No 'witches' had ever survived the grotesque drowning ritual in Carsden. There were no witches. All there was was superstition. He had entered a community where such beliefs still lived on. The mines had closed. Who was to blame? Abstracts such as economics and investment? You could not shake your fist at them. Better to find a scapegoat instead. That was what they had done. An unfortunate accident had marked Mary Miller physically as an outsider. Misfortune had dogged her publicly. She had been the perfect brunt. Darroch grew angry as he pretended to read. What could he do? He felt like rushing to the woman's house and asking for her forgiveness on behalf of the whole town. He wanted to speak with her, to see her. She was endurance. She was Christianity. He was a sham by comparison. He had to tell her these things. He had to tell her not to be afraid. Her eyebrows were like lines of velvet or the backs of sleek black cats. Her face was pale but deft. Her hair was silver. Silver and black. He had to tell her. He had to see her.

Reverend Walker had told him that Mary did not

work. Darroch put on his jacket, switched off the fire, and slammed shut the front door as he left.

He examined the character of the town as he walked. It was different now, different, certainly, from that first day when he had looked over his church with pride and hope. Raindrops dotted his shoulders, but he paid them little heed. They refreshed him.

It was a longish walk, and the wind blew into his face all the way, as if trying to deter him. Pieces of grit were swirled around Main Street and some picked at his eyes. He bowed his head into the gathering wind and walked on.

The cemetery stood at the top of a steep hill called The Brae. Her house was on the other side of the hill. Sweat was clogging his back beneath the nylon shirt, the woollen jersey, the jacket. He stopped for a second at the summit. The cemetery was quiet except for the cracked voices of the crows at Cardell kirk. He might pay Reverend Walker a visit while he was in the neighbourhood. He caught sight of a figure tending one of the graves. No, not tending it, but sitting in front of it on the damp grass. Her hair was unmistakable. He opened the gate to the cemetery and walked across the grass towards her. As he approached, he heard her voice. He realised that she was speaking to her dead parents. He stood stock still, numbed. Her voice was low and soft, like small sticks travelling with the river's current. He hung back, not wanting to eavesdrop so publicly but doing it anyway. Finally she stood up, turning and seeing him. A quick rising of blood made her cheeks glow against her wind-pinched face.

'Oh,' she said.

He was, however, more embarrassed than she. He opened his arms in contrition. A horn sounded at the gate. She looked past him and he turned towards the sound. A man was waving from the car. She waved back.

'I must be going,' she said. 'My boyfriend. The car.' She pointed, then started off.

'It was nothing,' he said with mock heartiness. 'I was just passing and thought I . . .' She was waving back at him, smiling warily. Then she reached the gates and the car door opened from within. Darroch let his arms fall, then pushed his hands safely into his jacket pockets. She would think less of him now. He had been spying on her. Her graveside. Her parents. He looked at the marble, at the gold lettering. She had been speaking with them. It was the most private of things, and he had blundered in like a . . . a . . . Her boyfriend. She had a boyfriend. Perhaps, then, she felt happiness too.

So why did Iain Darroch feel dejected?

Only two people had seen the boy and the tinker-girl as they picked their way hand in hand through the fields, the rain like a sheet behind them and the sky the colour of a deep purple bruise. One of these was Matt Duncan. He watched from the country path at the end of his evening walk, and his eyes were deeply focused slits. He felt his brain stir with incoherent thoughts. He slouched his hands into his jacket and cursed.

The other was Mrs Fraser, who owned the local grocery shop. She was on her way home, having delivered some produce to Reverend Walker. He had kept her late as usual, talking about the old days and the new minister. She had been walking home past the field next to the old hospital when she had seen the two shadowy figures on the other side of the wall. They were whispering together and giggling. She stood on tiptoe to see them better. They were past her and could not see her, but she saw them well enough and her mouth opened in a small O as she recognised the boy. She vaguely remembered having seen the girl, too, and knew her for what she was. Dear oh dear. Mrs Miller (she called her Mrs out of propriety's sake) was a good customer. Mrs Fraser would have to tell her about her son's unsavoury friendship. She would tell her first thing in the morning, for Mrs Miller was always bright and early in the grocery so as to avoid the mass of shoppers. A girl from the gypsy camp. Well well. Perhaps it was to be expected. Wait until the town found out.

They ate the evening meal in near silence. Sandy was happy enough. His thoughts were on how to broach the subject of Rian to his mother. Should he play on her sympathy, or should he come right out with his request? He was so full of his own concerns that he did not notice his mother's anxious face, the

216

way she glanced at him and only played with her food.

At last she rose from her chair and collected his empty plate. She walked to the sink and began to run the hot tap. Sandy belched in his seat. He studied his mother's back. Her hair was tied in a thick bun above the nape of her neck. Tufts of black ran down either side of her neck and disappeared into the shadows of her dress. He wished his own hair was as attractive, but it was becoming slightly greasy, and he could do nothing with it but let it take its own shape and its own line. He scratched at his neck.

'What happened to your grandmother's shawl, Sandy?' She had turned the tap off and was facing him, her hands on the rim of the sink behind her.

'What?' He knew that the red was already rising to his cheeks. His heart was like a sports car. It had just been let loose along a long, straight road. Oh shit, he thought. Oh shit.

'Did you give it to her?'

'To who?' His mother's consequent laugh was unpleasant. It had the hacking quality of a witch's triumph. She did not smile.

'To the tinker, of course. Your girlfriend.'

'Look, Mum, she's . . .'

'I know what she is! Everyone in this town knows what she is. But they all try to ignore it. It doesn't really concern them. And now you've gone and got yourself mixed up with her. How could you be so stupid?' The final word was like a judgement of fire. Sandy's face burned as brightly as a tongue of flame.

He had never, never seen his mother so angry and so disgusted by him. It was hard to hear out the rest of her verdict. 'She's just a slut. You've been lucky, Sandy. You've managed to gain some kind of acceptance in this town. I've worked hard for it. It hasn't been easy for you, and it hasn't been easy for me, and now you're going to throw it all away because of her. That's stupid. There's nothing clever in it at all. It'll be all round the town by now.'

'So?'

'So? I'll tell you so. Don't you think it's hard enough for me as it is without people laughing at me because my son's going out with a hoor?' There were tears forming in the corners of her dark eyes, so suddenly alight.

'She's not a hoor!'

'Oh? What is she then? You tell me.'

'She's . . .' It was impossible. All his pretty speeches, his arguments and his statesmanship had flown out of the window. His brain was soggy. He was up against a cruel and professional opponent. He felt cut, winded, leaning on the ropes with nowhere to go but back into the centre of the ring. 'She's like us,' he managed. His mother opened her eyes wide in astonishment. She laughed again, cutting him deeper.

'Like us? How dare you. She's a slut. She's not like us, Sandy.'

He wanted to play a cruel trick then, wanted to say 'So who's my father?', but he could not make himself do it. He swallowed hard. In the silence, his thoughts seemed to have struck home anyway. His mother came and sat at the table.

'Mum,' he began, his face pleading, 'I want her to come and stay with us.' He might have been asking to share his mother's bed. Her eyes only opened wider. 'Listen, I can explain. Rian's not what you think . . .'

'Worse then.'

'No, better. She's been used, that's all.'

'Used? I'll say she's been used! And everyone knows it. At least she's not fooled you there.' The sarcasm lasted only a second. She was looking at the table, was studying the texture of the sauce bottle. Her fingers played with the salt-cellar. The tears, their assault having failed, retreated. 'Sandy,' she said calmly, taking several breaths of air, 'please promise me that you won't see that girl ever again. Promise me that and things will be all right. You'll see.' He stared at the false love on her face. It was useless. He needed time. She wasn't giving him any. He pushed back his chair, not hearing its horrible scraping across the linoleum floor, and left the kitchen, climbing the stairs as noisily as he could.

In his room he lay on his bed, face down, and closed his eyes on everything: on his mother, on Rian, and on the small, tight world into which he had been so mysteriously born.

5

On his birthday, as planned, Sandy boarded the early train to Edinburgh. His mother had given him fifteen pounds. He had taken the money quietly, thanking her as politely as he would have thanked a distant aunt. She had been quiet, too, but had refused to weaken during the several fights that they had had in the past fortnight. He had even said that if his mother would accept Rian into the house, then he would return to school to do his Highers. She had shaken her head. Blackmail, she had truthfully called it. School had started three days previously. Secretly, Sandy was tempted by Highers. His friends had found nothing waiting for them outside school. Whether he liked it or not, he had until Christmas to decide. He knew that when he joined them it would be to a cold, flat world of quick-setting adult cement. Already Mark and Clark were bored, and were calling him 'lucky' because he could return to the womb-like warmth of the school with its ancient radiators and its sarcastic teachers, teachers like Andy Wallace, who had tried talking to him about Rian and his mother, but who had been a flabby, impotent interrogator.

Now he had money in his pocket and was sitting

on the old train, an engine pulling three carriages of second-class compartments. He was not intending to spend much of the money, only enough to satisfy his mother. The rest he was going to use to tempt Robbie, for he had not given up his plan. Instead he had modified it slightly: Rian and he would leave Carsden together, or Rian would hide out somewhere away from her brother and her aunt. The former was a drastic measure. The authorities would seek him out. They would be a wanted couple. He was not sure nowadays that melodrama like that could work outside of Hollywood films. Still, the alternatives were few and unsatisfactory. He watched Carsden swing away from him like a ball on a rubber string. It was rapidly replaced by spent countryside and indolent cows. Electric pylons swept across the landscape like giants, and he watched their rhythms from his window. The train seemed to pass a lot of back yards, as if it were an inspector of the shabby reality in every town. Rubbish strewn in gardens. Factories and warehouses with their rusting cast-offs. Earth-moving equipment at work right across Fife, and a petrochemical plant burning in the pale, smoky distance.

He considered the possibility of someone outside throwing a rock at his window. What would he do? He would not duck, just as he had not attempted to dodge Rian's slap. He would sit and watch the rock's trajectory cutting towards his reflection. His eyes would close over the splinters of glass. Why would he sit there? To experience, and so that afterwards he could curse his maker for creating the incident.

He believed in God now, but it was a malevolent thing and he would speak of it with a small, vehement 'g'. He believed in god. He believed in the cruelty and the inevitability of suffering. And he believed that he was doomed. As if to reassure him, thunderclouds gathered above the Firth of Forth. The train passed over and through the red structure of the bridge in a mist that hid from view the road bridge and the water. He knew that it was all because of him.

Soon enough, Edinburgh presented itself to him as a grey smothering of tall buildings. He walked up the steep incline from Waverley Station and was confronted by roadworks and fumes and a slow drizzle. He made towards Princes Street, one hand in his pocket so as not to lose his tiny roll of money. The city's coldness was a physical thing. People brushed past him without noticing. No one nodded or acknowledged his existence. Soon he was soaked. The drizzle was fine, but the traffic blew it into his face as though he deserved no better.

In a café, he was overcharged for a can of lemonade. He clutched his pound notes more carefully. The large shops were like nests of vivid ants. The streets were strewn with litter and curious men who asked for money or slouched on benches. Tourists walked by slowly, seeming not to see any of it except what they were there to see. Sandy began to wonder if it were real at all. He bought two records cheaply in a shop in South Clerk Street. Everywhere shops were being closed down, redecorated, and opened again. Many of the windows were boarded up. FOR SALE signs cluttered the immediate skyline. He found himself in a small concrete square. People sat on the steps around this square and talked. They seemed quite young, though a few years older than him. It was quiet all around. The road curved away from the square at a decent distance. The buildings were a mixture of the very old and grey and the very new and white. He ventured into one of the newish ones. It had a glass dome, beneath which sat a clump of tropical plants and trees. Music played in a café. There was a bank. Two other sorts of shop were closed. By reading various notices dotted around, Sandy was able to conclude that he was in a part of Edinburgh University. He was startled. He looked around furtively, but no one seemed about to throw him out. He walked out of the building and crossed the square to another, older construction. Inside, it offered much the same facilities as the first. They were like small, self-sufficient communities. For some reason they reminded him of Carsden. He wished that he had brought Rian with him. He wondered why he had not thought to ask her. He had not seen much of her in the past weeks. His mother had scared him off, but he had not given her up. He had not had enough money to bring her with him; that was all. He needed more money. Robbie, he felt, would never agree to let her go for less than thirty pounds. Sandy had only twenty-seven pounds fifty, less what he would spend today. He squeezed his pocket, wishing the money would grow.

He sat in the building for a long time. He ate a

sandwich in the empty cafeteria. It was peaceful in there. He did not want to leave but the train home was in less than an hour. In a good bookshop near the University he bought a book of poems by Ted Hughes, whom he had studied at school, and a novel which he had heard about somewhere. Then he walked down to the station, getting lost twice and having to ask directions twice. Once, he could not find anyone who knew anything about Edinburgh and he ended up asking a news-vendor, from whom he felt obliged to buy an evening paper, though it cost him another sixteen pence.

The train was crowded with people going home from work. He had to stand in a smoking compartment, and began to feel sweaty and sick from the fumes. The people seemed used to it all. They read their evening papers or their books and never talked or looked at their neighbours. Sandy, clutching his books and his records, could not read. Instead he watched from a small piece of available window as the thunderclouds over Fife churned and churned their way towards the interior.

6

George Patterson watched the empty, wind-lashed streets through the grimy window of the Soda Fountain. He had counted the day's taking, a pathetic sum. He had been thinking of the approaching winter. He could not face another one. He was thinking now of Carsden, of the town it had once been, of the man he had once thought himself. He was in ruin, like the town. He had lived a life that had been nothing less than a direct damnation for over sixteen years. He had sinned grievously. He had lied, had cheated, had watched his foulness push its way into the hearts of others in the deceptive guise of smiling acknowledgement, and he had detested every minute of it – wondering when his lies would be revealed, hoping and praying that they would, but never having his wishes granted. Wondering when he would crack, when he would reach the final edge of the final pit, stare deeply into it, and resolve the crisis. That stage had been reached. He had spent this last day ticking off the tumours in his life, an act of worthless self-excoriation that he had performed before, but never with the same resolve. Takings could be no lower. The summer was over. His life could be measured out by the half-empty jars of sticky, indeterminate things on his shelves. He was full of self-pity, and the only way to end his hypocrisy was the easy way, and the most difficult.

He went through to the alcove and swept up the trimmings of hair from the day's two appointments. He tipped the lot into a bin and stood the brush against the wall. Then he went into the tiny back room, where a bottle of whisky was wrapped in thin brown paper on the desk. In a drawer of the desk sat three small bottles of assorted tablets. These tablets had challenged him before. Now he felt equal to their challenge. He wagered the whisky against their success. He sat at the table, took a sheet from the drawer, and began to write in a childish, antiquated script.

It had rained all day and all of the night before. The river had burst its banks and flooded the park to a depth of nearly twelve inches. Part of the main road to Lochgelly was also flooded, though not quite impassable. Water gathered at roadside drains and waited patiently to be consumed. People were saying that they had never seen rain like it. It had fallen like a judgement in sheets of thick silver and black. Now it lay in the gutters and in pools, and people inspected it as if seeking the force that had been evident in its falling. But it was broken now, seeping back into the land as though its purpose had been fulfilled.

Broomsticks might be hanging in the sky. You could not say for sure that they were not. It was certainly dark enough up there for them.

But it was not Hallowe'en.

There were no whooping children, no turnip lanterns reeking, no outlandish costumes. Yet Sandy, walking silently through the drying streets, was thinking Hallowe'en thoughts. Chap, chap, chap, we are the guisers. That was the song for Hallowe'en, the witching time. But this was only the end of September. Hallowe'en was a long way off. He walked nervously past houses where he was known. He listened to the blaring televisions and arguments in every house, the arguments reminding him of those he had been having with his mother. Yet he had signed the options for Highers. He had not told her that, but he was sure that Andy Wallace would have. Homework begged to be done now, but his mind was full of Rian.

Today he had stolen a pound from his mother's purse. Three days ago he had done the same thing. His guilt echoed in the arguments around him, and beyond these sounds lurked the conspiratorial silence of the distant night air, mocking him for what he was about to do.

But he would do it, for he needed the money. He had stolen, he had scrimped, he had done everything he could think of. Everything except this. He shivered. It had to be tonight. All he needed was confidence. He was walking towards Cardell, towards where Rian lived. There were new houses there, incomers who did not know him. He was not the witch's son to them. He fingered the tin of boot-polish in his pocket. The dimmed light from venetian blinds showed him his targets. And suddenly he thought again, I'm too old for this, much too old. I'm too old and it's too early and it's stupid. Stupid, stupid, stupid. He rubbed at his brow as though worrying a headache. It was for the money. He needed the money and he needed it tonight. The money for Rian. He was so close now, and yet this gaping distance confronted him. He sighed. For the money then.

He crouched beside a hedge and took the tin from his pocket. It was half empty. His mother used it on her black leather boots, he on his school shoes. It smelled of warm kitchens, of fruit in bowls, making him even more uncomfortable for some reason. He dabbed his hand into the tin, smearing the thick polish over both cheeks and his nose, all the time forcing himself not to think about the minutes to come. Then, having wiped his hands on the edge of the pavement, he took off his jacket and turned it inside out. When he put it back on it was orange and furry with arms of cotton-white. It would have to do.

The house reared in front of him, looking bigger than ever. He stood at the gate, feeling sick, feeling his heart pounding with fear. Then he remembered that it was only a Hallowe'en prank after all, and he shuffled up the path towards the imposing wood and brass of the door. He stood on the doorstep for a long time, not thinking, just standing there. When some-one finally walked through the hallway he panicked, thinking that they were coming out and would find him standing there suspiciously. He thought that he had his story ready, so he pushed the bell. The person in the hallway stopped, put something down on a table, and opened the front door.

It was a man in his early fifties, dressed for an evening in. His slippers were furry-brown and well used. His cardigan hung loosely about him. He wore glasses and had a silver moustache. Sandy suddenly remembered that it was not Hallowe'en and that he was strange to the man in his strangeness.

'Well?' said the man. Sandy was purple-faced and hoped the polish would disguise the fact. 'Well?' Two mugs of coffee were steaming on a small telephone stool behind the man, and on the wall next to them hung an ornate mirror in which Sandy caught glimpses of himself. He looked like a tinker. 'Well?'

'Penny for the Guy,' he stammered. The man stretched to look outside.

'What Guy exactly?' he asked. Sandy stared stupidly towards where the man was looking. He began to remember his story.

'I've not built it yet,' he said. 'That's why I need the money.' *Need the money for Rian.* 'It's going to be the biggest Guy in the village. I'm having to start it early, you see. It's for charity.' The final lie made him lower his eyes guiltily to the doorstep. He had been talking too quickly, he realised. The man chuckled.

'That's fly,' he said. Then: 'Margaret! Come out here for a minute!'

There was a tortured, smiling silence until a fat woman, knitting in hand, came to the door. Her husband made room for her. Between them hung the mirror.

'Well,' she said, 'someone to see us.' Her voice and her face were ripples of condescension.

'He's a guiser,' explained her husband, 'but he doesn't have a Guy. That's why he needs the money. That's why he's more than a month early in calling. It's for charity, he says.'

Sandy hoped that his own silence would force the money from them. He wanted to run from their doorstep, and was prevented from doing so only by the thought of their laughter.

'And will we see this Guy when it's finished?' said the woman.

'Oh yes,' said Sandy. He watched himself in the mirror. He looked a bit like Robbie, though dirtier. The comparison attracted him for a moment until he realised that the woman had spoken again. 'Pardon?' he said.

'I said can you do something?'

'Do something?'

'Aye,' said the woman. 'Sing something.'

'Sing something?' he echoed, looking to the man.

'Is it a boy we've got here, Margaret, or is it a bloody parrot?'

They both had a good laugh at that, bending over slightly. Yes, he looked a little like Robbie, hard and unmoving.

'I can't sing,' he said.

'Well,' said the woman, 'tell a joke then.'

'You're a bit old for this, son, aren't you?' said the man.

'You must be able to do a dance at least,' said the woman, shaking her fleshy bulk like an aunt at a wedding reception. 'Go on.'

Sandy stared at his feet. They were monsters, infected with elephantiasis. He moved one of them out of curiosity, then began to do a little shuffle. He gazed at himself in the mirror. He saw a scruffy adolescent with jet-black hair and his coat inside out doing a stupid jerking dance on a strange doorstep. He forced himself to think of Rian, but it did not work. A solidity was gathering in his throat. He thought again of running, of turning on his heels and flying up into that beautifully clear night air. His audience smiled and clapped their hands in time to his movements, standing back a little into their doorway for a better view. The man began to whistle. The woman hummed in a broken-down voice, her hips moving obscenely. Sandy was appalled. He stared at them like a bear on a chain, and they were clapping and whistling and tapping their feet and humming along with the rhythm. He came to a furious stop. They stopped clapping.

The man examined Sandy with sudden depth.

'You're not much good at this, are you?' he said. 'You're not much good.' He chuckled. It was not a kind sound at all, Sandy realised. Children could be heard in the distance. The thought of money was all that held Sandy there, and he wanted to blurt out the truth to these stupid people, these warm, happy, stupid people. He bit his lip thoughtfully, hoping it would be interpreted as a sign of stubbornness. When he looked into the mirror now he saw a resolute face, a face anonymous and to be feared. He liked this look. He stared hard at the man. The woman had stopped humming. She took her coffee uninterestedly from the stool. She clutched her knitting to her bosom.

'How much will we give him?' asked the man, turning to his wife. She shrugged, then looked for a second at Sandy.

'He wasn't worth much,' she said icily. Then: 'The programme's back on.'

'I *was* worth much!' Sandy called to her retreating back.

The man attempted a more open chuckle.

'Aye, you don't do much these days for your money, do you? That's the trouble with this country. As little as possible for as much money, that's the way of it. You're learning the ropes fast, son. Not too fast, I hope.' He was digging into his pocket. His hand came out in the shape of a small fist and extended towards Sandy, who opened his own palm and received the chinking money without looking at it.

'You don't half talk a lot of shite, mister,' he said, turning to go.

The man chuckled again. The sound of bats against a window pane, of candles being snuffed.

'Don't go casting spells now,' he called bitterly as he closed the door. Sandy's stomach did a single somersault, no more, and then he grinned at having forced the feeble old man into saying that. He took off his jacket and reversed it as he walked. He felt stronger now, different. But he could not go through that again, not for anything, not even for Rian, his Rian. He moved further up the hill, away from the noises of the children. He lifted some newspaper from the ground and spat on it, scrubbing it against his face. He opened his warm, grubby hand and counted nearly fifty pence. Fifty pennies only. But he had gained something else, something that oozed from him as he rubbed harder and harder at his cheeks, enjoying the harsh, bright pain. Fifty bright pennies for Rian, his Rian.

So he had twenty-four pounds and eighty pence with which to tempt the gypsy.

FRI There seemed to Darroch something religious about Mahler's Fifth. He listened to it while sipping dry sherry, the glass absurdly small between his fingers – strong, hair-glazed fingers. He had finished Sunday's sermon. His sermons – full of disguised morals, and some not so disguised – had been warmly received by the congregation, none of whom, however, sought to put them into practice. He felt frustrated. What else could he do? He scribbled in the margin of the sermon, which was balanced on his knees. If only he could summon up the courage to speak with the woman in some depth, then he could fathom the extent of the town's feelings towards her. Yet each time he spoke to her he felt himself choking back the words and the feelings. It was absurd. Her eyes made him totally unable to say aloud what he felt so intensely. He was becoming obsessed by her. He did not want to think of it as love, and decided instead that it would only be cured if he were able to make himself talk with her about her life in the town. That, however, only led him back to his initial dilemma. There was emotion in Mahler's piece too, and emotion in the warming sherry. He felt them acting on him like chiding, agreeable friends. They put their arms around his shoulders and whispered, snake-like, in his ears. The room surrounded him like mortality itself: oppressive and inescapable. He shook himself free of these growing abstractions. It was time to be rational and clear-headed. He thought of the long walk to Mary Miller's house, and decided to take his car. The flooding between St Cuthbert's and Cardell was not too bad. He would manage to get his car through, God willing.

She wept for the first time in a week. She had resigned herself to the gulf which had opened out of nowhere between Sandy and herself. She had watched Andy as he had explained the reasons why he felt it best that they separate for a while. She had watched him make his apologies and leave her house, the house of her parents and of her grandparents. She had felt the world collapsing in on her. She had walked in a dream to the telephone box, but had not been able to get through to Canada. Now she was in the dreary graveyard, and, the grass being too wet to sit on – no, that was not the reason – she stood by the grave of her parents. She formed words in her head. She opened her mouth once or twice but produced only a dry clucking sound. Then she wept. She wept and she sniffed back the tears into her eyes, not wanting to waste a drop, and she wept again. She stared through the blur at the engravings on the headstone. She read her father's name. His age at death. The tiny sentiment at the bottom. Then she started to speak. She spoke to her mother alone, and the story she told would make her father disappear from everything for ever.

'I've lost him, Mum. He's decided that we should not see each other for a while. You know what that means. The coward's brush-off. It wasn't his fault though, Mum. No, he tried. It was me. I wouldn't have sex with him. That was the problem. It's a big problem with me, Mum, but I've never told you about it, have I? It's embarrassing, isn't it? But shall I tell you why? Shall I tell you what I could not bring myself to tell Andy? Dear Andy. You'll hate me, Mum. You'll hate me for eternity.' She blew her nose. The sky around her was darkening. Street-lamps suddenly came on outside the cemetery. 'You always thought that it was Tom, didn't you, Mum? It wasn't. People here believe that it was Tom too; I think even Sandy believes it. You know that he has never asked me seriously who his father was. I would never have told him anyway. But I'm going to tell you, Mum. Lord knows I've kept it bottled up for too long.'

She paused again and pulled her coat around her, though the evening was milder than the day had been. Sandy had given one of the shawls away, one of her mother's shawls. She could never forgive him for that. He had given it to that bitch of a tinker. And after all she had done for him . . . 'Sandy,' she said.

'Sandy.' Then she collected herself. She was here to speak with her mother.

'You remember that day, Mum. It was Boxing Day. You were going to Auntie Beth's in Leven. I said that I wasn't feeling well. Tom and Dad had arranged to meet with friends in the evening. So you went by yourself. I really thought that you were leaving us then, I mean leaving us for good. But you came back. I thought that Dad's drinking and his depressions were becoming too much for you. I know, he wasn't really to blame. The pits were all closed or closing and he didn't have much money left, or much of his pride. It was hard for everyone, wasn't it? There were always excuses. But when you came back, and when I told you later that I was pregnant, you thought it had happened on that night. You were right.'

A car passed on the road outside. It was a brave body who was driving on a night like this.

'Tom was out most of the night at a dance, then probably with that girl he sometimes saw in her front room. I was upstairs lying in bed, but dressed. I heard Dad and George Patterson come in. You remember, Mum, that they were very friendly. George Patterson was with Dad the night he died. It was suicide, you know. I figured that out right away. It was suicide that night, and George Patterson has had the guilt all on his own shoulders ever since. I've done nothing to remove it. I hope his life's been hell!' Her voice, at first uncannily calm, had now built towards minor hysteria. She tugged at her coat, staring over the wall of the graveyard at the clouds beyond. 'They were drunk and noisy downstairs. I could hear glasses falling, and then a bottle rolled across the kitchen floor. It's funny how those details stick in my mind, but they do. I can remember some of what they were shouting, too. All about the death of the town and the death of the workers and the death of pride. High-blown stuff. Self-pity mostly. They shouted and laughed and grew angry. They cursed the system and the bureaucrats. They cursed the NCB. They cursed just about everything but themselves. Dad did most of the shouting, didn't you, Dad? George was just backing you up. He had little enough to worry about. His shop was doing nicely. He was like a tiny fat king in a sugar palace. But he grew angry with you anyway. I couldn't stand it. By that time I really did have a headache. I crept downstairs.

'When I entered the living room it was like walking into somewhere for the first time. It seemed to have changed utterly. The chairs had been moved, and the settee. Some glasses were on the table, some others were on the sideboard, and two were on their sides in the middle of the room. A cardboard box half filled with cans and bottles of beer was on the floor. I remember it all so clearly. And a bottle of dark rum stood beside another of whisky on the mantelpiece. Dad had his arm round George Patterson. They were swaying in the middle of the floor, circling round the box. Dad saw me first. His hair was plastered down over his forehead. Sweat was hanging in the folds of his throat, or it might have been tears. His shirt-tail hung out over his trousers. I'd heard him that drunk before, when I was lying in bed sometimes, but I'd never *seen* him that drunk. Although I was looking at my father, I knew that I was dealing with someone else, someone with a different voice from the person I knew and with a different look in his eye. He came up to me and put an arm around my waist, but it wasn't funny, Mum. I slipped away from him and went and sat on the settee, arms folded. I was scared, yet I wanted to be in on it, do you see? I wanted to be part of their grown-up, men's world. I was fifteen, remember. I was already on the edge of that world. So I acted like a grown-up woman. Stupid of me. I sat on the settee and scowled. And Dad slumped down beside me and asked for a kiss from his daughter. He brought his face near mine and kissed me on the lips. It felt obscene. His face was bristly, and it scratched me. But he held me there for a few seconds. Then he pulled me to him again and kissed me again, not a dad's kisses this time but adult things. He was talking too, talking about the waste he had made of his life, and how I was the only thing he really lived for, how he had always cared more for me than Tom. He was stroking my back, and his breath was rancid. I thought he was all I had. I thought you'd run away. I suppose I was a bit sorry for him, but not much. I was sorrier for myself. He grasped me hard, pulling me towards him all the time. His grip was tight, a real miner's grip, and I fell against him. Oh, Mum, that was it, you see. It all happened then, and Patterson was there too. But Dad was half-hearted. No, I'm not telling it right.'

She paused. Her throat was dry. She scooped up

some water from a puddle and lapped at it like a dog. She felt she was going too quickly; none of it seemed plausible.

'I don't really know what I'm trying to say, Mum. It was so long ago. But later, when Dad was sick and had to go to the bathroom and collapsed there, well, Patterson. He did it. He did it. And it was against my will all right, but I was confused. I hit him, but he was a big, heavy man. And he was talking to me, but differently from Dad . . . He was trying to talk like a boyfriend. It was horrible. Talking about maybe getting married. Eventually I ran upstairs and sat with my body against the bedroom door in case they tried to get in. I was awake all night while they slept. It was disgusting, Mum, but how could I tell you? How could I? I don't know why I'm telling you now.'

She wiped tears from her face. Her breath was heavy. Her heart was a slow machine, rusted. She looked again at the ground, at the broken flowers in their jars, at the earth which held the two corpses.

'Oh, Mum, I don't know, I really don't know. But that's why Dad committed suicide. Because . . . I'm not even sure if he knew about Patterson. Probably not. So all the guilt was on him. But now all the guilt is on Patterson, you see. And though I love Sandy with all my might, still I can't help feeling sometimes that part of him belongs to someone else, someone I hate. Oh, Jesus, help me. You see now, Mum, don't you? And I couldn't tell Andy. If only I could tell Andy. Tom had nothing to do with it, you see. Nothing at all. He was mystified when he found out.

He thought it might have been one of his friends. Oh, Jesus, how can I talk to you again, Mum? How can I make you listen? I'm sorry. But it wasn't my fault, Mum. It wasn't my fault.'

She breathed deeply, her face to the cast-iron sky. Rain was falling somewhere, and soon would fall here again. She walked quickly from the cemetery, her coat around her like a rough skin. A car had stopped at the gates, but it was not Andy. There were to be no miracles. It was the minister. He walked around the car towards her. She was elsewhere, but he could not see it.

'Miss . . . Mrs Miller, eh, I was just coming to see you. I didn't catch you at your house so I . . .'

'Go away, will you? Just leave me alone!' She began to run downhill. She did not know where she was going, but she knew that it had to be some-where lonely and somewhere uninvolved. In the end, she ran towards the flooded park.

Robbie was blind drunk. That much Sandy knew by just looking at him. The young man was slumped against the outside wall of the mansion. He cradled a near-empty bottle of vodka in his arms and sang to it as if it were his baby sister.

'Oh ho,' he said as the boy approached. 'It's Sandy, is it? Will you sit down here and have a drink with me, Sandy?' He waved the bottle in Sandy's general direction. 'You will have a drink, won't you? I'm hellish lonely these evenings. You stopped coming to see us. What's wrong?'

Sandy crouched in front of him. With one hand he

steadied himself on the ground, while the other hand stayed in his pocket, where the roll of notes lurked.

'Listen, Robbie,' he began, staring at the bleary slits of the young gypsy's eyes, watching the eyes themselves glisten and roll and pull themselves into focus, 'I want to speak to you about Rian.'

'About Rian? Ha! That little bitch? Don't let's speak about her, Alexander. Let's enjoy ourselves. Here.' He motioned towards Sandy with the bottle. Sandy took it from him and gulped down the vodka. It burned in his throat, but made him feel better.

'Yes,' he continued, 'about Rian. I've got some money together, Robbie, and I want to . . .' Robbie's head rolled.

'Money,' he said, 'money, is it? Oh yes,' he rubbed at his chin and a little wise old man's face came over him, 'the money. Rian told me about that. You're supposed to be getting together some money. What for again? Oh yes, to buy her from me. Ha! That's a good one! *Buy* Rian! As if *she* could be bought. She *can* be bought, mind you, but not like that. No, not like that at all.' It was as if he were talking to himself. His eyes stared at the gathering dusk, seeking answers to unspoken questions, then were dragged towards the ground by the weight of the alcohol. 'No, Sandy, you can't buy Rian. It was a trick. She told me all about it. Told me to keep quiet. But you're me pal, aren't you? I'll tell you. It was her idea, Sandy. Nothing to do with me.' He shook his head vigorously, but his eyes fixed themselves on the sky. 'Rain. Any minute. Anyone can see that.

More fucking rain. It's damp in that house. Why does nobody ever come to fix the roof? The tarpaulin's all torn or worn away or something. The ceiling is rotten. Not fit to live in. Not fit. Ah, but Sandy me boy, she was taking you for a ride. Not her usual ride, but a ride all the same.' He laughed at the gods. It was the sound of drunken jubilation. It would be forgotten by morning. 'Taking you for a ride, my son. She wanted me to grab the money, then neither of us would have anything to do with you afterwards. We'd board up the windows proper, or disappear, and never see you again. What could you do, eh?' He shrugged his shoulders. 'Nothing. Unless you were prepared to tell people that you had been planning to buy yourself a gyppo girl, and who'd have sympathy for you then, eh? No-fucking-body. Not in this town, Sandy. So you'd be up the creek, right? Without a paddle, right? But never fear. Your old pal has told you. He's saved your fucking neck, so sit and have a drink with him. Sit yourself down.'

He patted the ground beside him. The grass was sodden. Sandy could feel it underhand. His heart was racing. He understood now, and he believed. It had been stupid all along not to. Robbie, Aunt Kitty, his own mother – they had *known*, they had instinctively known the rottenness that was core deep, for they had lived through it themselves in many manifestations. Yet she had been loving towards him, gentle, fragile. Could it possibly have been merely a game, a charade for her own benefit? Robbie was speaking again.

'You're awful quiet, Sandy. Did you fall for it

then? Did you really save up all your pennies? So have others before you. You're not alone. Have you come here to give all your pennies to Robbie? Do us a favour and go get another bottle instead. Keep the change. You can have the bitch for free, but I doubt if you'll be able to take her.' He grew less animated. 'She makes good money sometimes, and when she does she gives me some for a little drink. To keep me quiet, I suppose, and so I'll look after her and protect her from the big wide world out there. But I'll let you into a secret, Sandy. I'd look after her anyway, without the bribes and the booze. She's my sister, you see, and I've been looking after her since I was a kid.' He waved his arms in an uncertain sweep. 'How much did you bring, Sandy? Fifty pounds? She said you'd manage fifty, said you had some nice things in your house. Myself, I said I doubted whether you'd get more than thirty or thirty-five, but she was adamant that you'd manage fifty for her. She said you were that much in love.'

'Shut up!' The final syllable racketed around the garden and in Sandy's ears. 'Shut the fuck up!'

Robbie put his hands comically over his ears, grimacing, letting the bottle slip to the grass. Sandy remembered that he was only a few years younger than the gypsy. He reached out and slapped Robbie with his free hand. The feeling was shocking, but satisfying too, as if he had done something really wicked against authority: dropping litter or shitting in the playground. He touched his stinging palm with his fingertips. Robbie rubbed at the spot of red on his grey cheek. He was not going to retaliate.

Sandy wondered if this were the same strong, cocky person whom he had encountered in a shadowed room only a few months previously. It was like watching a cancer victim growing old too quickly. It was like watching his grandmother as she had wept herself towards death.

'Where is she?' he asked. His voice was firm like a film actor's. Robbie shook his head. He was studying Sandy's feet now.

'Could be two or three places,' he said, still drunk but trying not to be. 'Could be down by the river in the park, but it's flooded, isn't it? Sometimes she takes them to the back of the swimming pool. Other times it's behind the Miners' Institute.' He shrugged his shoulders. 'It's no use, though. What could you do? Nothing. Better leave her alone, Sandy. You'll only hurt yourself. I don't want my pal hurting himself. Stay here. Come on, we'll finish this bottle and get another. Nothing's to blame really. Just, well, everything. This fucking town. This fucking country. Anything you want to blame.' He shook his head wearily. 'Stay here, Sandy. It's getting cold. We can go inside, if I can get up the bloody pipe. You can wait for her inside. Look, look,' he put his hands out, palms upward, like a slouching Buddha, 'look, Sandy, it's beginning to rain again.'

But when Robbie looked up, Sandy had vanished. He peered into the gloom, but saw nothing.

'Sandy,' he said. 'Sandy, you'll only . . .' Robbie slid sideways down the wall and was asleep.

She was not at the Miners' Institute. He walked on,

down the hill towards the swimming pool. It had been a gift to the town from the miners, built in the mid-1960s when things were already beginning to turn sour. It had been popular throughout Fife for a time, but then a much larger pool had been built in Kirkcaldy, and another dream had become merely an echo in the showers. Now it was used by the town's swimming club and by some old people. It was falling into disrepair. Gangs painted its walls with vaguely sectarian slogans and would gather against its back wall to be warmed by the hot air ducts there. Some public conveniences, much vandalised, stood locked nearby, and the park was separated from the pool only by the town's bowling green.

Sandy took a short cut behind the bingo hall, wary of the shadows. The Cars might not be far away. He could easily fight them all on a night like this. The slap he had given Robbie stung in his memory.

The rain hardly touched him, and his eyes stared at the backs of the buildings. It looked as though someone had broken into the Soda Fountain, but that was of no concern to him. She had been cruel. She had been needlessly cruel. Every fibre of her was rotten with experience. She might burn in hell, but she would have to face him first. His fingers tightened into hardening fists.

Mary walked by the edge of the flooded park. Her shoes were sucked at by the sodden grass, but she could not feel the dampness rising around her. She had stopped crying, and had set up the necessary barriers between herself and her grief. She would survive, but she wished that the night were over. She wished that she could transport herself many weeks into the future, to a time when everything had healed and seemed to have taken place in an unreal time. Either that or let her fade into the long past, beyond the Boxing Day to a time when the world had promised much and asked for little. She stopped to look over a railing. The stagnant, near-dead burn had filled with rain-water. It was as if it had been revitalised. For a moment she might have been ten again and watching Tom playing football. She remembered that day. The goblins in the burn. Her burning hair. It was dreamlike now, as this night would sometime be . . .

Sandy heard the animal sounds and recognised them. His stomach like a sea-squall, he turned the corner. She was against the wall, moving with a forced motion up and down it. A duct hummed above her and sent a small amount of steam curling down over her and the figure which obscenely wedged her against that rough wall. He knew that figure. It was the worst thing he could have imagined. The grunts were unbearable. He watched in fascination as the rhythm played itself out. He almost laughed. It was banal; like adults playing at being children. Then he walked towards them. Her head turned and she saw him approaching. She pushed at Belly Martin, but his weight was on her like heavy winter blankets. His head rested against her as he eased himself down towards reality.

The reality was stunning. Sandy pulled him off Rian by the hair, lank and greasy, away from the unresisting girl. He threw him, grunting, against the wall, turned him, and kicked him solidly in his absurdly babylike genitals. The squeal was satisfying. His fist sank into an unfeeling, doughy mass. He stood back and kicked again, and Belly Martin squealed again and went down on all fours to be sick.

Sandy, breathing lightly, looked at her. She had smoothed her skirt down and her head was bowed, her lips red and bated.

'Slut,' he said. It was as if he had hit her. She jerked a little, but kept her eyes on the ground. He saw that she had the shawl, grubby now and hanging heavy with rain, around her shoulders. He did not want to touch it. Suddenly he felt subdued, tired. His brain was tired and his legs were tired and he wished that it would end. He eased himself against the wall beside her and rubbed at his forehead. Boot-polish still hung in the air around him, the grubbiness of gypsies. She had not moved.

'Sandy . . .' Her voice was quieter than Belly Martin's retching. 'Sandy, it was Robbie . . .' He shook his head in disgust.

Belly was cursing him with what breath he had. Sandy pushed the obscenity with his foot and watched it roll over. It curled itself into a foetal, protective position, rather like a snail, and did not move.

'Sandy, it's not like you think.'

'No more tricks, Rian. I've been too fucking stupid

247

for too long.' But then why was he listening to her at all? And why was his head thumping like some tightened drum-skin? He should leave now. He should make the best of it. What was the best of it? He levered himself from the wall and moved past her. She put a gentle hand on his back.

'No, Sandy, listen to me. It's you I want, Sandy. It's you.'

When he turned she was right behind him, and she stood forward even then to kiss him on the lips. Her tongue ran along his teeth, her hand snaking to the back of his neck, caressing the headache, the tension. He felt her cool saliva. How much of it, he thought with sudden revulsion, was Belly Martin's? He pushed her away, but she fell against the wall, steam wafting around her. Graffiti encircled her like the frame of a painting. Her hands were behind her back and inviting, the whole of her body open to him. He faced her and felt triumphant, a warrior claiming some prize. But she was . . . He should . . . There was no sense . . . Her hand went to his thigh. He was a child again, staring at what he did not really understand.

Then he heard the scream. He had never heard his mother scream before, and yet he knew that the sound was hers. It lasted only two seconds, but it was his mother, and he knew that it was coming from the park. He turned away from those wide, knowing arms and began to run.

It had been a miracle, as if God had ordained it. Here she was, delivered unto him, at his mercy. She had

248

had no mercy, and he would show none. Poor George. What had she done to him? She had bewitched him, as she had bewitched others. She had destroyed Matty, and now she had destroyed George. There was no one left in his life. They had been systematically taken by her. She had put a blight on the town and on his own life. Poor George.

He had gone to the Soda Fountain late. He had told George that he would not be coming at all, but had managed to anyway. The door was locked. It was strange that it should be locked so early in the evening. He had knocked, but to no avail. He had walked round to the back of the shop, peering on tiptoe through the small, blackened window into the back room. George was hunched over his desk as though writing. He had tapped on the window, then had knocked and called out, but nothing had moved inside. Only then had he seen the bottles. He had put a stone through the window, had opened the catch and strained towards the bolt on the door. He had pushed his way inside. His friend was cool, growing cold. He could not believe it. An envelope lay beside him, addressed to Mary Miller. In his stunned grief Matt Duncan had torn it open. He had unfolded the note.

Mary, you will never forgive me, I know, and will feel that, in some ways, I've taken the easy way out. I have suffered all these years, believe me. I have suffered. Perhaps you are satisfied. Perhaps satisfaction does not enter into it. But I hope that you can find it in your heart to forgive me. Please forgive me. Your father's last words before he died were 'I loved her, though,' and I believe that he did. We are not bad men, Mary. Only very stupid.

So, she had driven him to his death, the bitch. The witch. He had been infatuated by her. There was evil in her. Evil. He had called for the doctor and had given a short statement to the local policeman, Sergeant Jobson. Then, left alone to his misery, he had walked down to the park. And there she had been, delivered into his hands.

He approached her from behind, his shoes splashing water. She appeared not to hear him. Her hair was tied in a ball behind her. He grabbed for it, trembling.

'Murderer!' he spat out. 'Bitch. Murderer.' She screamed then as he forced her head down, her body following, towards the water. There was a slight splash, as of bath-water, as her head sank. He pushed her in further, his legs becoming wet and his face spattered with rain. She was not really struggling, though. Her hands beat down in the water, but she was not really trying. He held her strongly, his face twisted with the effort. He fell on to his knees, still holding her down. He felt justified at long last, and released from his ancient burden.

Her mouth brushed the grass. Her nose was pressed painfully against the ground, but that was the only real discomfort. Her eyes opened on darkness, yet just above her must be dim light. Her hair stung with

250

the memory of it, as if she were only now living out the dream of all those years ago. The grass was a living thing beside her. It caressed her and spoke to her in bubbles of emptying air. Her whole front was saturated – she was becoming part of it. She wanted to release her last breath and finish the act, but something held her back. She could not tell what it was, but she knew that it was working against her will. Her hair flamed behind her, each strand calling out for peace. If only Sandy and she . . . If only . . .

Then, with a sudden jolt her hair was free and floating, and the pressure on her head and back fell away. She rose from the shallow pool like a fish on a thin, strong line and saw, through the water streaming down her face, the old man humped like a camel while the young boy played on his back. It was comical for a moment. Then she realised that the man had just tried to kill her, and that the boy was her son. Sandy was shouting at the man as he wrestled with him. Her ears drained and she could hear his cries.

'Leave her alone! Leave my mum alone! Leave us alone!'

He thumped on the man's silent back and kicked at him. She noticed that he was looking very grubby, as though he had just come out of the Wilderness. She did not understand what was happening, not exactly, but she saw Sandy's bright teeth gritted in determination, and she knew that whatever he was thinking, it had to do with endurance and even perhaps, just perhaps, a kind of resurrection.

THE FLOOD

Ian Rankin's first published novel, *The Flood*, introduces
themes that later will be taken to another level with the
Rebus series. Mary Miller is a happy child until the day
when, victim of some nasty horseplay, she falls into the
'hot burn' and nearly drowns. But worse is to come when
her lustrous dark hair turns silver overnight – and
thereafter the superstitious residents of Carsden can only
wonder if she's been touched by witchcraft, especially
when it seems as if divine retribution has come into play
with the freak death of her tormentor Matty Duncan. And
rumours abound further several years later when Mary
mysteriously falls pregnant, her brother Tom escaping to
Canada soon after, while her father turns first to drink
and then to an untimely death himself under the wheels
of a car one foggy night.

Fifteen years later Mary's loving son Sandy
compensates for her difficult life and, tentatively, Mary
even asks herself whether the attentions of kindly
schoolteacher Mr Wallace might mean there could be
happiness in her life after all. But unbeknown to Mary,
Sandy has been bewitched by the charms of a local tinker
girl with debatable intentions, and is planning a very
different future. As local sweetshop owner George
Patterson tries vaguely to watch out for Sandy, it becomes
clear that with the many types of 'psychological jousting'
going on, secrets are layering upon secrets, and soon
Andy Wallace understands that there may be an unequal
struggle to win the hand of the woman he loves, just as
Sandy discovers he may lose everything he holds dear.

A terrible flood threatens Carsden, but this is nothing compared to the tumult of disaster that's about to rain down. As two essentially good people battle the odds, Ian Rankin shows how dangerous secrets can be, and how pernicious superstitions and suspicion are in a small community.

Discussion points for *The Flood*

What is Ian Rankin saying about the difficulties of escaping one's past?

He has described *The Flood* as 'a young man's book, all about the perils and pitfalls of growing up'. What do you think he means by this? And, thinking about narrative techniques and characterisation, how might this show in the way the book is written? Under the aegis of being a 'young man's book', how successful is Mary Miller and what happens to her?

According to Ian Rankin an aunt was allegedly so perturbed by reading *The Flood* that she was left 'crying for my soul'. Should she instead have been crying for the souls of the characters in the story and, if so, for whom exactly? To what extent, if any, are we to bear in mind that *The Flood* is set against the background of a close-knit, religious Scottish community?

How seriously is the reader meant to take the actual story? Do you think Ian Rankin means what he says to be taken absolutely literally, or as (in parts at least) a long-running metaphor? Is there a slightly fairy-tale feel to the narrative? If so, is this because of the way in which various literary allusions might have been employed?

Arguably, *The Flood* has the most melodramatic plot to all of Ian Rankin's novels. Would it be fair to claim that his subsequent move into more realistic storytelling enabled a deeper and more complex discussion of important issues?

How does Sandy feel an 'outcast from society', and might this be in part why he's drawn to Rian, who is excluded by others just as much as he is? Perhaps most importantly, why has he never asked Mary who his father might be?

'He was a sinner, so maybe nothing would happen. But then, he thought, all the more reason for God to want to save him.' Sandy believes this about himself, but might Rebus agree too? Where does Ian Rankin stand in *The Flood* regarding notions of 'sinners'? Is he connecting the flood to ideas of baptism, mercy, redemption and resurrection?

Does Ian Rankin succeed with the characterisation of George Patterson and Matt Duncan, who are much older than the author was at the time of writing? And what is one supposed to make of the Reverend Iain J. M. Darroch, MA, BD?

Reading Group Notes

The Flood has an unashamedly rural setting. In comparison with how Ian Rankin later exploits the urban aspects of Edinburgh, does the country setting offer more limitations or more freedom? Is the political comment on the decline of the mining communities in Scotland implicit or explicit? In later books, do you think it is fair comment to say that Ian Rankin tends to offer political or social criticism through his characterisation rather than simply through polemic, as here?

What themes can you identify – such as, say, the fuzzy boundaries between good and evil – that will later be the basis of many of the Rebus books?

Ian Rankin claims that *The Flood* is not a crime story. But is it a mystery, or perhaps a thriller? Discuss the pros and cons for both sides of the argument, and whether the way the reader is fed information about the characters influences this sense of the kind of book it is.

Describing Sandy, Ian Rankin says, '*Today he was part of a group, a gang. He would walk differently and talk differently and act altogether differently. Walking to the bus stop, they had fed from each other as if studying older men*.' Although the description alludes to a group of teenagers embarking on an innocent day out, can the reader avoid superimposing thoughts of other, less innocent gangs who will appear in the author's subsequent books?